Nobody Checks the Time When They're Happy

Nobody Checks the Time
When They're Happy

Eun Heekyung

Translated by Amber Kim

WHITE PINE PRESS / BUFFALO, NEW YORK

White Pine Press
P.O. Box 236
Buffalo, New York 14201
www.whitepine.org

This work is published under the support of the Literature Translation Institute of Korea (LTI Korea) and with public funds from the New York State Council on the Arts, a State Agency.

Book Design: Elaine LaMattina.

Cover image: *Lemon with Knife, Pinball, Handcuffs and Pocket watch* by Hall Groat II. 11 x 14 in. Oil on stretched canvas. Private collection in Cocoa Beach, Florida. Used by permission of Hall Groat II, Professor and Chairperson, Art and Design Department, SUNY Broome Community College. WWW.HALLGROAT.COM

First Edition

Korean Voices Series, Volume 24

ISBN: 978-1-945680-08-3

Printed and bound in the United States of America.

Library of Congress Control Number: 2016960874

Contents

An Obviously Immoral Love

I once read a short story where a man announces to his shocked family that he wants a divorce and is about to walk out the door when his son hurls a can at him, knocking him unconscious. The man lies coma-stricken in the hospital, incapable of divorcing his wife or of marrying his younger lover. Everyone else—the son, who almost killed his own father; the wife, betrayed after twenty years of marriage; and the other woman, swept up in forbidden love—is stricken with unhappiness. The story ends with the author returning home to brood over the unfortunate family. Which member of the family does he write about?

Me

Three years ago, when I was twenty-nine years old, I stayed up every night and slept in late the next day. It wasn't a peaceful sleep, though, because sunlight and traffic noise spilled into my west-facing window every morning. I spent those mornings tossing and turning in bed. Every day for nearly a year, I told myself to get curtains for the window—*I'm putting up curtains today no matter what!*—but when night came, another day had passed and still no curtains. I was always alone, and it was always dark.

I lived in an old apartment building surrounded by high-rises. Small offices were crammed into my building. On the lower level, a café and a bar waited eagerly for the evening rush of after-hours clientele. Seedy bars and street stalls lined the back alleys. A four-star hotel standing next to an eight-lane highway was the most respectable building in the area. Across from the hotel stood another stretch of gray, shabby buildings.

The streets seemed to suffer from insomnia like I did. Cars came and went; people ran into one another and just as easily left. Cars and people swelled the streets then disappeared, leaving in their wake a silence that lulled me to a fitful sleep.

I always kept a bag of rolls in my fridge. There were ten rolls in every bag. Every day, the bag shrank by two rolls. On the fifth day, I would, without fail, discover mold on the last two rolls and throw them away. Along with the moldy rolls, I sometimes threw away months-old, long-ago-soured *kimchi* my mother made for me. She came to Seoul every three months for her regular physical at a clinic for menopausal women. Every visit, she brought fresh *kimchi* that sat ignored in my refrigerator, souring in a bag proudly labeled "freshness guaranteed." She sometimes came to Seoul to attend someone's wedding, and when she did, she'd get upset with me for not having married, but she knew her scolding had ceased to have any effect on me.

On the last day of each month, I went to the bank to pay the bills and deposit money into my savings. I always bought a box of Kotex on the way home. I had an extremely regular cycle—every thirty days. I could tell when a new month was about to start by when my period ended. Sometimes, I'd arrive at my door, turn the key in the lock, walk into the empty apartment, and feel a wave of loneliness. When that happened, I knew it had been more than a week since I'd talked to my mom on the phone.

I woke up every morning when my cuckoo clock chimed eight times. The clock was broken and perpetually twenty minutes behind. After a shower, I got ready for work and stuffed my sketchbook into a black, flat portfolio. I worked at an art studio located on the ninth floor of a sixteen-story building across from the hotel. I left for work with my long, curly hair still wet, secured with a clip.

Out on the street, I'd fall in step with the crowd and without realizing it, start walking faster. In just a couple of minutes, I'd arrive in front of the hotel, where I'd wait for the light to turn green before being thrust into the crosswalk. Soon, I'd find myself in front the elevators in my building. Waiting for the elevator, I'd let out a deep breath that I'd been unconsciously holding in. I stood there with a blank look on my face, dully staring at the bank offices located on the first floor.

I worked with my friend Kang, who'd hired me and two other designers. We had regular work, designing book covers and illustrations for several bimonthly corporate newsletters. Added to this were print ads, catalogues, and leaflets, which made for a good amount of work. Despite the workload, Kang always complained that there was barely enough money to cover the salaries for the four of us. The Kang who ran the studio—which doubled as his home—was older and more haggard than the Kang I used to know, whose real passion was painting. He likened his fate to that of an unappreciated genius and was miserable that it had been years since he'd sat before an easel.

The year I graduated college as a French literature major, my father's company went bankrupt, forcing me to give up my long-planned study abroad in France. After that, I took classes in print design, hoping to find a job. Since then, I hadn't listened to a single *chanson*. Unlike me, however, Kang wasn't numb from desperation. He still held out hope for an escape, so he was always full of energy.

"We got a contract for a book on health called *Grape Therapy*. I need you to go down to Chungmuro and find the best pictures of grapes you can find, grapes covered in dew, for the cover. As for *Restructuring Korean Companies*, I think we can do it all on the Mac. Two drafts should be enough. We can use the stock photo of skyscrapers we used for *Economic Revolution*. Just change the title. When are we getting the proof for *Husbands: Friend or Foe?* When you pick up that proof, make sure you get the photos we edited," Kang ordered.

When I took notes, I usually unfastened the clip from my hair and let it fall. Running my fingers through the dampness, I shook my hair loose, releasing the smell of shampoo. I used my free hand to stroke my hair. When I was on the phone, I doodled endless rows of G clefs or drew birdcages on the backs of used Xerox paper.

The year I turned twenty-nine was also the year Kang started staying up late more and more often because of work. I arrived at the office to discover empty plates of take-out food on a tray outside the door, covered in newspaper. Walking in, I'd ask, by way of wishing him good morning, "Did you pull an all-nighter again?"

Kang's pointy chin seemed permanently covered in stubble. He'd recently formed the habit of gazing long and silently at the coffee mug he kept perched on his knee, his hands cupping its warmth, and muttering, "At this rate, I might never make it to India..."

However, he managed to leave for Calcutta that spring.

He said his plan was to tour India for two months but then added that plans change. Without Kang, there'd be no one to find new clients for the studio. No one would be there to whine about how hard it is to pay his employees when he doesn't even have time to shave. The rest of us would be left on our own. My income would no doubt take a hit, but I knew I could get by for three, even four, months if I dipped into my savings. As for what happened after that, I'd think about later. My father's business was struggling again, so I wasn't going to ask my family for help. In return, I expected them to not meddle in my life.

Before he left for India, Kang dragged me to a meeting of the India Dreamers Club where he was a member. After the meeting, we all went to a bar, where I was introduced to the other members. One was a high school teacher and poet, and another was a plastic surgeon based in the suburbs. There was also a bank manager who, like me, was there for the first time. Dressed in a dark green polo shirt, he smoked Dunhills and spoke in a low voice. In that low voice of his, he told me he'd seen me before.

"You were in an elevator, carrying a flat, black bag," he said.

"That could have been anyone." I brushed him off. "I have that bag with me now, but it's fairly common. As for elevators, they're in every building."

He smiled. "Do you think I'm lying?"

I was thinking that his fingers were long and slender. I waited as he crushed out his cigarette in the ashtray and the embers faded to black. But he didn't speak again.

It was late by the time we left the bar. I was the first to walk out to the street, where the air hung heavy with the pungent smell of flowers and garbage. He followed me outside. I sensed he was slowly edging closer. Suddenly, he brought his fingers up to my hair.

"Your hair..."

Before I could turn around, the rest of our group, having paid the check, poured raucously out to the street.

Kang, drunk, peered left and right, ostensibly looking for me. Staggering over to where I was, Kang spotted him standing next to me. Playfully, Kang slapped him on the shoulder and began talking like they were old chums.

"Your name's Han, right?" he slurred. "You know, I happen to know your bank. Know it very well. Those leaflets on your installment savings plan next to the tellers' windows? The ones with the three golden eggs hanging from a tree? I made those, you know." After a beat, he went on, "So now you're working at headquarters?"

"Yes, I work in foreign exchange," Han replied softly.

"Look at me! I'm introducing myself to you and I haven't even given you my card..." Kang muttered as he fumbled in his pockets. In a few days, he'd be leaving the address stamped on his business cards, so he was about to give the man an address where he couldn't be reached.

"When are you planning on returning from Calcutta?" Han asked Kang.

"I don't know," Kang replied. "Never, I hope. Here's my card. Our office is in the Mapo District."

I had a friend who, having decided that relationships were too painful, announced one day that she was leaving her old life behind. She was going to a Buddhist temple to become a nun. On the bus ride there, however, she sat next to a soldier and ended up marrying the guy after two months. It seems the people who denounce relationships are the very people who long for human contact. They attempt to escape, all the while searching for a way to attach themselves to something. That is the essence of all human solitude.

Because the buses had stopped running, I took a cab. Han hailed it for me, which felt surprisingly natural. My thoughts briefly wandered to him as the cab sped through the night.

His Woman

Until recently, Han had worked at his bank's Mapo District branch. That's where he first noticed the woman with the flat, black bag standing in front of the building's elevators, gazing vacantly into the bank. One day, he asked his wife to bring him some paperwork he'd left at home. On his way down to the café where his wife was waiting for him, he saw the same woman walking toward the elevators. He followed her into an elevator going up. It was just the two of them inside. She unfastened the clip that held her long, curly hair. As she shook her hair out, he smelled the scent of her shampoo. As soon as she stepped off, he pressed the button for the first floor. He forgot which floor she got off on, but the smell of the shampoo stayed with him long after.

He told me this the day I had the abortion.

"Why are you telling me this now?" I asked.

Without a word, Han stirred a bit of salt into the bowl of beef soup he'd ordered for me. We were sitting quietly in a nondescript restaurant. With his chopsticks, he added a generous amount of chopped scallions into the soup, murmuring, "Scallions are good for you. Eat."

By then, I'd learned he only spoke when he wanted to. I knew better than to prod him. The beef soup was a little salty. He'd seasoned it to his taste. Sometimes, what we do for others results in an imposition of our ways on them. I tried to focus only on his good intentions and bear the rest in silence. In love's early moments, the urgency of wanting to prioritize the other person's needs over our own keeps our inherent selfishness at bay. That's why I sat there and ate the salty soup in silence. It was the same reason I later followed him to a bar against my better judgment.

We sat at the bar, looking out at the street through the large glass windows. Each time the traffic lights changed, pedestrians took off from either end of the crosswalk and met in the middle of the eight-lanes. Their movements resembled the way blood circulates in our bodies, replacing old blood with the new. Han drank nearly half a bottle of Scotch. A few streaks of his white hair caught the light from the overhead halogen lamps and glittered like the silver scales of a snake. His wrinkles cast deep shadows. *What's he thinking about?* I wondered. Perhaps he'd already made up his mind about something and was only assuring himself that he'd made the right decision. He looked exhausted.

I sat with one hand propping my chin, the other playing with a yellow straw, slowly stirring a glass of lemonade that had turned lukewarm after the ice melted. Was I supposed to feel that day was worse than any other day? I'd been careless with myself—that much was true. For that, my body and mind had both suffered, and I'd have to bear the moral implications of what I'd done. But if I had to suffer from a guilty conscience, it wouldn't be for the abortion—but for my love. Immoral is what I chose to be the moment I fell in love with him. What I couldn't bear wasn't the experience of the abortion but the love that would still be there afterward. What was painful was the knowledge that if I really wanted to escape this pain, what I needed to do was get up and leave him for good, forever—instead of sitting at this bar staring at a glass of Scotch and wallowing in the sappy emotions left over from the excitement of the day.

I noticed people pouring out into the streets. The bars were closing.

"Should we go?" I asked. Han took the Dunhill he'd kept balanced between his fingers and extinguished it in the ashtray. But instead of getting up, he held his gaze on me.

Once, he'd told me how his wife had argued that as far as she knew, all bars close before midnight. So on those nights he came home past one in the morning, she punished him as if he'd stayed out all night. When Han and I said our goodbyes for the night, the first thing he did was to turn on his pager and phone. He started his car in a hurry, his palms sweaty from a sense of urgency and from the effort of concealing this urgency. I never asked him to stay with me longer. On the contrary, I felt a kind of peace once he was gone, as if I were decompressing after a long day at work. If he could have an okay marriage, that would be great for him. Would I have gotten jealous of his wife if I thought loving him meant I had to steal him from her? No. Our relationship had nothing to do with getting married, getting a job, getting a promotion, or any of the other to-dos everyone is expected to check off their life list. I never demanded anything from him.

Back when I was still taking design classes, I once participated in a sports match with the other students. The next day, I woke up sore all over. I was told it was because I'd used muscles I don't normally use. Muscles I wouldn't have known existed were causing me pain. In the same way, he and I were feeling an unfamiliar sensation—pain—in the muscles we'd long abandoned, like people who haven't exercised in a long time.

He parked his car near my apartment building. We walked slowly toward my place. As I walked, I felt something wet and soft slip out between my legs. The nurse had said, "Since you had your procedure today, today is the first day of your menstrual cycle."

Ever since I got my first period at the age of fifteen, my periods had always come on the last day of the month. Now, I'd have to expect it in the middle of the month. My body had abandoned the rules it had kept since birth and succumbed to new rules derived from our relationship. A woman's body must be programmed to remember the past.

"Why am I telling you this now?" Han repeated my question as we waited for the elevator. "When we first met, I immediately recognized you as the woman with the shampoo smell. To me, you're more than just another woman. You're special."

He let out a deep sigh. "I don't know how much longer I can run from this..."

Ding. The elevator doors opened. He got on first. "Let's go."

I didn't move. He'd never been inside my place before. He usually walked me to the elevators then took the stairs to the parking lot. "I said let's go," he repeated.

With one finger on the button to keep the doors open, he grabbed me by the arm. "I'm spending the night at your place."

And, before I had a chance to come up with the right words to say no, he added, "I'm asking you to marry me."

I opened the door of my studio to the forlorn cries of the cuckoo bird that had been left alone in the dark. Like a sobbing child that's finally found someone to listen to his cries, the bird cuckooed a couple more times before it scurried back to its home, the doors closing shut behind it.

"Is it midnight?" Han asked. I explained, "The clock's broken. It's twenty minutes behind."

His hand reached underneath my sweater. My breasts, which were sore this morning, were no longer sensitive to the touch.

"I can't tonight."

"I know. I just want to sleep next to you," he whispered. "Will you change my life?"

Utterly exhausted, I fell into a deep slumber. Waking up during the night, I was surprised at how natural it felt to see him sleeping next to me. I guess shame was an emotion that was lost on me. There were imprints on his cheek from where he'd pressed it against the pillow, and I could feel and smell his breath escaping between his lips. I caught myself tucking him in. I was shocked that I had such familial instincts.

I rose carefully so as not to wake him. I walked to the fridge. Inside, a damp chill choked the nearly empty bins. If he were home, what would he have for breakfast? I reached for a Tupperware of *kimchi* that, once opened, greeted me with a strong vinegary smell. I thought of the things people typically keep in their refrigerators. I thought of what my mom keeps in hers.

I never wanted us to get married.

But then, that might have been because the notion seemed impossible.

The next morning, he kissed me and left for work. His beard had grown a little overnight, giving him a haggard look. He might be described as disheveled, unkempt even. He'd certainly seem that way to his bank's female employees, maybe an employee who arrived at work early, changed into her clean, pressed uniform, and began merrily watering the potted plants kept around the office. Obviously, she wouldn't be the type to sleep with a married man ten years her senior.

That afternoon, he called me at work. He scolded me for not taking the day off.

"You're being stubborn. What did I tell you? This is why I have to take care of you."

I found myself scribbling "stubborn" and "care" on a loose sheet of Xerox paper.

"You're supposed to have beef bone soup and get plenty of rest after those procedures."

I scribbled "after those procedures." Next to that I scrawled "experienced," and circled the word many times.

There were many experiences which were my first but not his. When we first slept together, he reached behind my back and expertly unhooked my bra. When we showered together, he made sure to turn the tap to a light drip so the water wouldn't make too much sound. And I couldn't blame him for that. If I did, that'd be like begrudging him the experiences he had as a thirty year old, a thirty-one year old, a thirty-two year old and so on when I was still only twenty-nine. He'd had a life before we met. And his wife was part of that life.

No one, upon stumbling across great-tasting food at an unfamiliar restaurant, would jealously prevent others from discovering it. Rather, we love to advertise discoveries of this kind. The same goes for a beautiful view. No one would build a wall to stop others from enjoying the same view, except maybe ill-tempered giants in fairy tales. But the same isn't true of love. No one knows for certain how long love will last, which makes love exclusive. We yearn to possess it, and this urge begets obsession. This obsession has the potential to destroy love, but even with that threat hanging over us, we can't stop ourselves. I was no exception. I was slowly beginning to consider marriage as an option for us.

After he and I hung up, I saw that my coffee had gone cold. I put down the receiver and got up to make fresh coffee. As I did so, I noticed something written on a corner of one of the Xerox pages. *Vouloir, c'est pouvoir.* I don't remember when during the phone conversation I wrote those words, but they were definitely in my handwriting.

Once, while at the bank waiting for my turn, I saw a poster on the wall for a wanted fugitive. The drawing was of a man with a narrow forehead, handsome features. *WANTED: Prone to wearing glasses and disguises and speaks in Seoul dialect. When in panic, reverts to the rural dialect of Jeolla Province.* I smiled wryly thinking of that as I reached for the coffee filters. What was it that threw him into panic, and what was he trying to hide with another dialect? To want is to have?

That night, Han came to my apartment again.

I let him in without a word.

He often said he wanted to change his life. He sighed and said that his real life was somewhere out there, ready for him to start living it. He said he was never fully present where he was, that part of him was elsewhere, with his real life.

"When I first met you, that desperation was at its peak. I was bored at work and at home, as if there were more to life…"

He tried to find himself by taking photographs of tranquil harbors and the famed fir tree forests of Mt. Odae. Realizing that he hadn't invested in himself as much as he should have, he splurged on several camera lenses. But he soon tired of this hobby. When one of his colleagues at work retired early and opened a café near a subway station, he showed intense interest in cafés. But upon learning that his colleague was renting space in a building owned by his father-in-law that would soon pass into the colleague's hands, Han grew tired of that idea as well. His wife called it a midlife crisis. Then she kindly suggested they participate in Bowling Wednesdays for couples. When he announced he was going to start attending the India Dreamers Club meetings, she encouraged him, even telling him about the Good Dads meetings for fathers interested in good parenting. When he drove to the countryside in search of a nice suburban house, however, she put her foot down and said she'd never live in a rural town. It made him feel lonely to know his wife's support was conditional.

One day, his wife took their only car to drive their kindergarten son to a nature camp for a field trip. It had been a long time since he'd gone to work without his car, so he grabbed a few drinks after work before getting on the subway. In the train, two college girls in front of him were busy discussing a guy one of them had met online.

"He messaged me, asking if I wanted to go for a drive."

"Whoa, for real? And then what?"

"I lied and said I had a car so I didn't need to go on drives. Then he created a chat room and invited me. Guess what the password was for the room."

"What?"

"S-E-X."

"Oh my god. Did you join?"

"No, but he kept messaging me, like, 'Hey, don't you like to have fun?' and 'Come on, meet with me, I promise it'll be worth it.' So I agreed to meet up with him, and guess what? He was this tiny little kid, still in junior high! I blew him off right there."

Han's ears burned. He glanced sideways, hoping to spot someone who could give these girls the tongue lashing he couldn't. The man to his right, who looked like he worked in a cubicle, had his nose buried in 99 *Ways to Win Over Your Boss.* To his left were a young guy and girl too wrapped up in each other's arms to notice anyone else. It seemed he was the oldest person in that midnight subway.

His house was in one of the newly-built cities outside Seoul, located one stop shy of the train's final destination, which meant he had to sit there with that sinking feeling in his chest for quite some time. At the subway exit, he slipped his ticket into the slot and was leaving the turnstile when he looked up to see a man on the opposite wall walking towards him. The man looked old and tired. Han kept walking, his eyes on the man. The man in the mirror also kept his eyes trained on him, eyes that were empty and hollow. Passing the man in the mirror, Han thought again of his age, forty years old—caught between the years he'd had and the years he had left.

"You're not going home tonight, either?" I asked.

"Doesn't matter." He fell asleep next to me.

Sometime around dawn, my phone rang. Quickly, I grabbed it and in a voice that was low but quivering with unmasked contempt for whoever it was that was calling so early, hissed, "Hello?"

The voice on the other end sounded just as tight. "It's me, your mother."

"Mom? It's so early..."

But before I could finish my sentence, she burst into tears.

My Mother's Daughter

Waiting for my mom's crying to subside, my mind raced, weighing all the ominous possibilities—*Is she sick? Did she lose money? Did she have a bad dream?*

Did one of our relatives die?

Even as she was telling me Dad had announced he was leaving her, my mind was too busy racing to process what she'd said. But then it hit me. *My dad was leaving.*

"He says he wants, just once, to live his life the way he wants," she sobbed. "He says he wants to be free... At least, that's what he says."

Had my dad found it unbearable to deal with her constant preaching and criticizing, all supposedly done for his own good? His announcement wasn't just another power play he was pulling to swing the tide of a fight in his favor. And to drive his point across, he hadn't come home that night. Mom stayed up all night, until the white light of dawn filtered in through her window. Whatever my dad had intended to do, he'd succeeded. Realizing this was serious, my mom was seized by a terrible rage.

"I know who his bitch is!" she screeched, her dull voice suddenly coming alive with potent force.

I kept one hand pressed against my forehead as her rant continued.

After what seemed like ten minutes had passed, I switched the receiver to my left hand. "I'll call you back," I said, and without waiting for an answer, I lowered my arm to put the phone down. But I couldn't remove my hand from the receiver, so I stood there with it in my hand. My long hair fell across my face. Sweeping it back, I realized Han was standing behind me. Holding me close, he buried his face in my hair and asked, "Who was that?" Sunlight was already streaking in. I gazed at the westward window. I felt his breath inching closer from the nape of my neck to my earlobe. It smelled faintly of cigarettes. The smell was familiar. I used to sniff it on my dad when I was little.

That night, I called my mom. My dad still hadn't returned.

"Ask anyone in the streets. What would a young floozy want with an old man like him? Obviously she thinks he's got money and is after it. Crazy whore. She's a fool to want to be a mistress!"

Her words rang with the pride of knowing she was not a mistress, but a wife.

The word *mistress* is quite effective; it can be used to denounce an unchaste, cunning, pitiful woman. In a quiet voice, I said, "That's what you say, mom, but you also told me she's a junior high schoolteacher in her forties. She's not in this for the money."

"Then she must be really crazy! Her husband died several years ago, but there were nasty rumors about her at work before that. I can't believe I have to put up with this. I have to fight a hussy almost half my age?"

"Fighting won't solve anything, mom."

"So am I supposed to sit back and see what happens? I could go to her school right now and rip her face apart, and I still wouldn't be rid of her!"

"If you do that, Dad's never going to come back to you."

I was sitting on the edge of my bed when I looked down and spotted a strand of hair on my pillow. It was short. And white.

"Why are you talking like this is none of your business? You're my daughter! You should be here with me instead of lecturing at me! I know another woman whose husband cheated on her. Her daughter took matters into her own hands. She even met the mistress!"

I imagined myself, heading to my hometown in an expressway bus. I get down from the bus and arrive at the café where I've arranged to meet the other woman. My long hair is tied in a firm ponytail, my mouth set in a determined line. I see her already there waiting for me. Even before I sit down, I glower at this woman, my dad's mistress. *Why are you seeing a married man?* I lift my chin, staring down at her. *Don't you care that our families will suffer?* The woman, after bearing my questions in silence, suddenly gets up. *You have the wrong woman. I'm not your father's mistress.* Shocked, I ask, *What? Who are you then?* Sneering, she replies, *I'm the wife of a man you know very well.* The scene goes white and zooms to a close-up of my confused, alarmed face. Suddenly, my hair comes undone and falls around me in long, curly clumps, making it ideal for getting pulled.

"I know women of her type," my mom was saying. "I don't have to see her to know what she's like. She's supposed to be a teacher of children, but she's doing the devil's work! It's obvious she has no shame, that she's a whore!"

I bit down on my lip. "It's also your fault what happened, mom."

"What? What did you say to me? My fault? How is this my fault? Believe me, men come up with all sorts of excuses to justify having an affair! Why, a girl can get pregnant out of wedlock and still give a million excuses!"

I let my eyes wander to the bag of pills on my table. The bag had a small green cross printed on it, next to which was written in blue letters, *Kim Young-Ok OB-GYN.* I kicked the table, hard. It dragged across the floor leaving striations in the linoleum. The lamp on the table teetered, its shade swaying. Nervously, I dug at a stack of paper with a pen, tearing the pages to shreds.

"Well guess what, he won't go through with the divorce. He's too old and backward. I know that man through and through and let me tell you, he won't do it!"

Despite the assurances, her voice was shaking. Suddenly, she unleashed a torrent of curses, not directed at my dad.

"Whore! She'll cry blood from her eyes in exchange for the tears she's made me cry! Just you watch what happens to home-wreckers. She'll lose everything she has! I'm not climbing into my grave before I see that hussy ruined and done for. I'll follow her to hell, I will!"

For a while, there was only the sound of heavy breathing coming from the other line. The silence from my end was equally intense. My shoulder was stiff, one hand wound tightly around the phone's cord. Now the shoulder shook. The emotions my mom and I were harboring in our respective silences were entirely different from one another.

After a long while, she finally spoke. "I have to go now. I need to eat something. My tongue feels so raw, I can barely drink water. But if I died now, I'd lose this fight."

I was about to put the phone down when I heard her ask, "Did you have bread for dinner again? You're just like your father. You're both picky eaters and lazier than lord knows what. Who'd put up with you and your ways?" Tears slid down my cheeks and fell on my knees. I drew back, startled that I'd been crying.

My Father's Daughter

I was just like my dad.

My mom's scolding annoyed me as much as it did him, although I knew that without her nagging, life would be a lot less manageable. Nonetheless, it was a ceaseless, irritating reminder of what I already knew was the right thing to do.

"Why do you always do your homework late at night?" She would bark. "Can't you finish it when you come home from school? Wouldn't that take your mind off it when you're playing? And why do you always play under that dim lamp? That's why you needed glasses at a young age. Why are you using a knife to cut those circles anyway? Why aren't you using scissors? Using the right tools saves time! You always tear at bags with your teeth when you could be using a knife or scissors. Look at your desk. It's a mess! No wonder you can't find your scissors. Women are like houses; it matters how you maintain yourself. Look at how careless you are. Who'll marry the likes of you?"

It was worse for my father.

"Will you please change your clothes as soon as you get home? Clothes are like people. You need to look after them properly or they'll get creased and filthy and you'll never get them to look decent. Look at you, you left your glasses on the floor again. Pay more attention to what you're doing! Don't you remember how you stepped on your glasses last time? Give me your shirt. Look at all these coins in your pocket! No wonder your shirt was dragging down. Didn't I tell you not to shove change into your pocket without counting it first? This shows how careless you are. Nothing's more foolish than taking the easy way out and paying the price for it later. You think it's convenient to stick your change in there but you'll lose more money in the long run. Where do you think you're going? Aren't you going to help the kids? Or go check on the weeds in the garden? Why do you always stay cooped up in your room like an invalid? What will the kids learn from you? And why won't this nasty cigarette smell go away? Stop! You'll scatter ash all over the floor! Didn't I tell you to see where your ashtray is before you light your cigarettes? Where are the deeds to our land? Did you get a copy of the land register like I asked? Let me see it. Where is it? Is it in your jacket pocket? Look at all these coins. How am I supposed to find the land register? What if the coins tear a hole in your pocket and you lose something important? These little habits can make a big difference if you can learn to change your ways. But no, you'll never change. Oh no, look, look! You got ash on the floor, like I knew you would! Where would you and the kids be without me?"

Whereupon he'd retreat to the bathroom and she'd bang on the door, yelling that he'd forgotten to take the ashtray again.

My dad liked to be alone. I don't know whether he'd always preferred it that way or if it was her nagging that forced him to withdraw into himself, although it's not important which came first. What's certain is he didn't shut himself away from the world like "an invalid," as my mother put it. He was optimistic and had a great sense of humor, and when he dusted off the old trumpet he used to play in his high school band, he beamed proudly, like a child. He liked to listen to classical music, despite mom's admonishing. ("It's just as they say, a man is only as good as his hobbies. But instead of doing something active, like fishing or hiking, all your father does is sit in his cave.")

One of my greatest pleasures was watching him build sleds and kites, as he was fairly good with his hands. That didn't please my mom.

"Stop watching him waste his time and go finish your homework!" She'd yell. But I stubbornly stayed by my dad's side. Once, when mom hollered at me to come to dinner, I clucked my tongue without looking up at her. For that, I had to suffer a tirade that lasted as long as it took me to finish my meal. But as I got up, I clucked my tongue at her again, and paid for it with a lashing.

My dad didn't respond to any her scolding. Unlike me, he could stay calm because his contempt for her drove him to silence. Only after I'd grown up did I realize this—that he held contempt for her. When I did, I grew to fear him. Despite the scorn he felt, my dad submitted to doing the right thing, which was to answer the call of duty as a husband and provider. Besides, he wasn't strong enough to remove himself from the familiar orbit of family and duty.

One day, when I was twelve or thirteen, I bought a bag of chips at a store. The chips were shaped like rings with holes in the middle, which made for a fun game where I could slip them on my fingers and bite them off one by one. I was coming home from school with several of the chips on my fingers when I ran into my dad outside the front gate. He was in a huff, his face twisted with rage. Suddenly, he lunged at my hand. Snatching the chips from my fingers, he threw them on the ground and stomped on them. My chips lay crushed on the ground, when just a second ago they were wrapped around my little fingers. I stood there trembling in fear and shock as he screamed, "Don't play with your food! You hear me?" I couldn't understand why he was so mad. It was hot that day and a drop of sweat was crawling down the side of his face. His neck was red as a rooster's comb and bulged threateningly against the stark white collar of his shirt. I went pale as a sheet and stood frozen where I was, stealing a few furtive glances at our house. I was old enough to know my dad was taking out his anger on me and that the real reason for his rage lay elsewhere. That day, I learned that good and evil can exist inside one person, but I was still at a loss when it came to dealing with the evil inside my dad. I couldn't work up the courage to burst into tears, much less cluck my tongue at him like I did at my mom. I was a coward, just like my dad.

And perhaps just like him, I don't know when to feel shame.

On TV, a new movie was just beginning. I'd seen it a few years ago on the same channel. It's about a married guy who falls in love with another woman while celebrating his fiftieth birthday at his favorite bar. As he's leaving his family to be with her, he says to his wife, "It's not you. It's just that, when I'm in this house, I feel like a faded calendar. But when I'm with her, I feel like I have a new life."

I stuck out my foot and using a toe, pressed the off button on the remote.

My second toe is longer than my big toe. I'd heard that people with longer second toes lose their fathers before their moms. My dad has longer second toes. His dad died before he was born, so in his case, the myth held true. Thinking of my dad's toes, I let out a long sigh.

I remember reading about a convict who was caught trying to escape prison a few days before his release. When asked why, he clutched his chest and bawled, *I couldn't stay in there a minute longer, let alone a few days.* When you've carried a burden for too long, it takes only the weight of a single piece of paper to bring it crashing down. Should I advise my dad to bear his burden until it collapses of its own accord? Should I preach about moral high ground when he's struggling under this weight? Teach him that betraying someone is wrong, but lying to yourself isn't?

In every family, the members have their teeth sunk into each other's backs. If they loosen their bite, everyone will scatter and the family will break apart. But if they bite down too hard, they'll rip each other apart. That's love.

The phone rang. I grimaced at its piercing shrill. After ten rings, I picked it up.

"Why'd you take so long to answer?" It was Han. "Who were you talking to for such a long time? I tried calling you from work but I couldn't reach you, so I came home. My wife's gone. She must be protesting my late nights out. She's probably at her mother's."

That night, it seemed the whole world was full of daughters and their mothers, women and their men, wives and their husbands.

He continued, "Now that I've made up my mind, I can't stay here a day longer. I'll be forty next year. If I don't do something now, I'll spend the rest of my life this way. You're my last chance. You know that?"

Outside, the noises of the city were in full swing. Cars came and went. People met and said their goodbyes.

"Do you think your life will change with me?" I asked.

"Yes."

"How so?"

"Because you're the woman I love."

"Twelve years ago, did you marry someone you didn't love?"

"I loved her then. I must have. That's why I married her. But it wasn't the real thing."

"Let's say you do marry me. Won't you be saying the same thing twelve years from now? You'll probably leave me when you get another 'chance,' thinking that 'chance' is the real thing and I wasn't. Like how you're trying to leave your wife right now."

"What is it you want to say?" he demanded angrily. "Just tell me the truth. You don't want to marry some old geezer and spend the rest of your life raising his kids. Is that it? You think I'm playing games here? What kind of jerk do you think I am? You've got a real hurtful way of turning down a man."

He hung up. He lacked the patience that usually allowed my mom to regain her composure before hanging up the phone, no matter how excited she became. I stared down at the receiver. I said to him the things my mom wanted to hear, and told my mom the things he wanted to hear. The two were fighting a battle inside my mind. I couldn't tell which side I was on.

I sat up and reached over to fluff the pillows. There were two more strands of hair. Both white. After throwing them in the trashcan, I took the pills from the ob-gyn. I turned the TV back on and sat stupidly in front of the screen, like a moth drawn to a flame. The movie was about to end. The guy had quietly shown up at his daughter's wedding and was giving her a hug. I knew how the movie ended. The dad joins the family for a group photo, as the guests applaud. After that, he goes back to his mistress. The mistress, who'd feared he might return to his family for good, tearfully wraps him in her arms.

The bird in my clock started cuckooing. It was 12:20.

I lifted the phone receiver, then put it back down. Reconsidering, I started dialing. It rang several times. *Are you sleeping?* I whispered to myself. *Pick up the phone. I need to talk to you.* The tone was about to sputter out when someone answered.

"Hello?" It was a woman. "Hello? Hello? Is someone there? Hello!"

I remembered how he once complained that his mother-in-law lived so

24

near that his wife thought she could get away with doing a sloppy job of the housework.

I hung up the phone, turned off the lights, and went to bed.

It wasn't my parents' issues that drove me to lose my temper at him, but because it was too painful to admit the fact that I couldn't marry him. Having missed the chance to tell him that, I tossed and turned all night.

My Mother's Rival

Mom called every night.

"Can you understand your father? He should act his age and live out the rest of his years preparing for his retirement like any decent man would. Instead, he insists on being with a younger woman, like he doesn't give a damn what society thinks!"

"Does it matter what other people think?" I asked.

"Of course it matters. That's what makes us people, by keeping up our reputations and not losing face. If you walk around with your privates hanging out, that makes you a dog, not a man. I found movie stubs in his shirt pocket the other day. I couldn't believe it. The only time I've been to a theater was when I went to the Nam Jin concert."

"Are you still going through dad's pockets?"

"I didn't do it intentionally! I only turned them out to do the laundry. What was I supposed to do? Can you believe that man? He can't stand me but he's fine with wearing the shirts I wash for him and eating the food I cook. Last night, that hussy called our house."

Dad had moved back in but he hadn't set foot inside their master bedroom. He'd come home late, sleep in the other bedroom, and leave first thing in the morning, after shedding yesterday's clothes. The only phone in the house was in their master bedroom, so whenever I called, it was always mom who picked up.

"What did she say when you answered the phone?" I asked.

"What could she say? The hussy hung up without a word."

Could it have been me she was talking about?

So far, I haven't been sympathetic to her cause. My mom thought I was as evil and ungrateful as my father.

"I'm not surprised. After all, you're his seed." Then she slammed down the phone.

The next day, she called back, not to pour out her woes, but because she was afraid of being alone with her thoughts. She was a lonely woman. Sixty years of work and errands had left her with no capacity to experience the luxury of solitude. *Mom, take it from someone who knows what it's like to be alone—solitude doesn't go away because you've shared it with someone,* I thought, but couldn't bring myself to say out loud. Instead, I said other things. "Dad has his own life, mom. He's outgrown you; there's nothing you can do about it."

And as she launched into a long, angry harangue, I thought to myself, *You can't force someone to feel a certain way. All dad wants is to be with the woman he likes. It isn't easy to fall in love at his age. Imagine how much he cherishes this. The more you obsess over him, the more he'll try to escape. Pretend dad's gone, and get used to being alone. Go on a trip with friends. Take up calligraphy. Volunteer at a hospital. It's not too late. Stop depending on someone else's emotions. Keep yourself at arm's length. You're the master of your own life, for fuck's sake!*

When an obsession takes over, we turn into a shell. We can't see anything, we can't eat anything. Strange how only the experience of crushing solitude can teach us the pitfalls of an obsession.

Kang sent postcards from Calcutta. "Now that I've put some distance between myself and Seoul, I can see things more clearly. In India, the pressures of the caste system are still very much alive and real, but the people are free. I find that strange. I have so many things to tell you when I get back."

I spent my nights doing one of two things. When I wasn't talking to my mom, I was with Han.

Once, we were sharing the pages of a local newspaper while waiting for our food at a restaurant. The title of a column by a psychologist caught my eye, *Why Married Men in Their 40s Prefer Young Women.* It said that, according to research, when married men have an affair, they prefer women who are ten years younger or more. These men have exposed their childish sides, their vulnerabilities, to their wives. Years of marriage have given them a shared life. By the time they reach middle age, the wives believe they know their husbands through and through. They treat their men like they're children. But the problem is that after they hit forty, men feel a growing urge to validate their existence. They become dissatisfied with the way their wives view them. That's why they turn to younger—much younger—women, who express admiration for their money, social status, and world experience.

The psychologist was right. This butch desire to be seen as real men is certainly one reason why men cheat. But some men crave the opposite. They want to go back to being a child. I've seen cases where older men lord it up as authority figures in their home then coo sweet nothings in a baby voice to their young lovers. After skimming over the column, I swapped my pages for the financial section.

Han devoured the piece on unfaithful men, probably thinking the arguments made sense. I disagreed. The number forty is just another arbitrary concept. So is "relationship with a younger woman." These concepts don't apply universally to everyone. They're like divinations; people who accept them to be true are likely to be influenced by them. Han never suspected that his dull, stoic conservatism was responsible for his dull, routine life. Instead, he tried to justify everything with a reason, including his love. However, he hadn't changed with age. He'd always been conservative.

Things with Han were as bad as they were with my mom. There were two ways he referred to his wife. I recognized the subtle difference when he referred to her as the anonymous pronoun *her* as opposed to calling her *wife*.

"You're sick of her, but you're dependent on your wife. You call her different names, but she's the same person."

"It'll be different with you. I'm not right for her, and she's not right for me."

"How am I different from your wife? We both tell you to cut back on drinking. We both tell you to switch to low-tar cigarettes. When I do it, you think it's considerate, but when she does it, it annoys the hell out of you. You say you don't want to be like an old calendar, but nothing ever stays new."

"You've changed," he'd say. "Don't you know what I'm going through? Why are you being so difficult? Let's go. Let's talk at your place."

"No."

"Why not?"

"I don't want us to go to my place."

"Why, because you might end up at the doctor's again? You think I'd let that happen to you a second time? No! That's why I want us to get married!"

On his way down to the parking lot, he asked wearily, "Did I put too much pressure on you? Do you really love me?"

I arrived home to find the phone ringing.

"Where were you all night? Don't you care what's going on at home?"

my mom screamed.

All through September, sheets of paper piled up next to my phones at home and work, scrawled over with doodles.

Other things happened, of course.

On the day Kang was to return from India, I got a call from my dad.

Kang's flight was due at 5:10 in the afternoon. The three of us from work planned to surprise him at the airport. After the others left, I stayed back to clean up the office. As I was turning the key in the lock, the phone started ringing. I was going to ignore it and leave, but it had started pouring and I suddenly realized I'd left my umbrella at my desk. Sighing, I turned back and lifted the phone off its hook.

"Hello?"

"Is this Art Vision?" my dad asked in the soft, reserved voice of a middle-aged man who'd spent his whole life providing for his family running a respectable small business. His lightly accented voice was wary, searching. I had almost no memory of speaking to him on the phone. Mom had always fielded our conversations, and therefore, enjoyed exclusive access to us both. Because of this, my dad and I remained severed, blissfully unaware of each other's problems. It surprised me when Mom said that I grew more like him the older I became. I knew the man so little.

"How are you?" he asked.

"Fine, Dad. And you?"

"I'm fine."

Even after I'd finished drawing lines across a page of paper and dozens of G clefs, both of us remained silent. I began drawing birdcages. My dad was probably tapping his pipe with one hand or ruffling through the pages of a calendar. Who knows? What I did know was that he, too, was searching for his next words.

"The reason I called is—" Clearing his throat, he started again. "I wanted to discuss your future."

"What?"

"Do you still want to finish your studies?"

Having made his start, his next words came rushing out as I blinked in surprise.

"What do you have to do to study abroad? I don't know how the process works. Is there a way you can pay the whole tuition in one lump sum, so you don't have to receive the money in wire transfers? I'm trying to put my affairs in order at work." He cleared his throat again. "I'll give you some money. You can use it to pay for your wedding later or go abroad and study. It's up to you. Would that be all right? What's your bank account number?"

Now that he'd given his reason for calling, he breathed a sigh of relief and added, "Don't get too excited though. It's not a lot of money."

Outside, it was pouring rain. I ran to the car idling by the curb. My clothes were soaked through.

"I forgot the umbrella again!" I complained loudly.

"I thought someone might have called you," one of my co-workers said.

"Yeah, it was my dad." I was trembling from the effort of concealing my excitement. I'd felt this way when Han proposed marriage.

After completing my course in design, I gave up all thought of studying abroad, but only because I knew it was impossible. Now, all I could see were the stairs I used to climb to get to my French classes at Alliance Français.

I was carrying a small purse instead of my usual big, flat portfolio bag. I took out a handkerchief and wiped down my wet hair. Almost mechanically, I wiped down the side of my purse. I flinched, catching myself.

Women need to keep clean and tidy the places that aren't seen. You ever see those women who parade around in nice clothes not realizing their heels are muddy? They probably wipe their purses only down the front where people can see, and forget to wipe the sides. Just like you do with your schoolbag. And when did you last wash your sneakers? Have they always been that gray?

After my mom delivered sermons like these, I'd angrily hurl my bag and sneakers across my room. But they always remained spotless.

Dad hung up after I gave him my bank account information. He didn't breathe a word about Mom. If they got divorced, I'd still belong to him and remain a part of his family, not of mom's. It was as if my mom had to become miserable for all my dreams to become real.

I learned at an early age that the world worked in a zero sum manner, where A's unhappiness equaled B's happiness: Kang left on his quest for freedom, so the rest of us had to pull extra shifts. But I'd never heard of a daughter who steals her mother's happiness so she herself could be happy.

I stared at the rain coursing down the car window. My eyes were seeing nothing, as unfocused as they were when I looked into the glass windows of the bank where he worked. Not realizing that my breath had long since fogged up the window, I stared until my eyes hurt. I had no intention of congratulating my dad for finally choosing to live the life he'd always wanted.

Kang brought back small Buddha statues and incense necklaces as souvenirs. We went back to the office, where he lived, put down his bags, and trooped downstairs to the bar.

He began a long, seemingly endless review of his travels. Park, one of the designers, tried to stop him. "Come on. It's been two hours! You know what I heard India does to people? After you've been there once, you can't stop talking about it for three months. After you've been there a second time, you write a book."

"And after the third time?" one of us asked.

"After the third time, you're left speechless."

When we settled in at our second bar of the night, Kang sat next to me.

"You don't look like you're having a good time. Is something wrong?"

Before I could answer, Park cut in with a joke. "How can any of us have a good time with you here?"

Kang continued, "No, I'm serious. Something's changed with her. Are you seeing someone?"

I scoffed and lifted my drink to my lips.

Someone else replied, "Seeing someone? Do you know how closely we guarded her while you were away? No one's called her today except her father. Right?"

Whenever I fell and scraped my knees, when I got a nail stuck in the sole of one foot, when I cried at the sight of my first period, I turned to my mother's warmth. Not to my dad and his cigarette smoke. Despite what he thinks, the peace and comfort he enjoyed for most of his life were possible thanks to that warmth. After all that, can he say he's gotten sick of her self-righteousness? Didn't he know it came with the territory?

Suddenly, I wasn't scared of my dad anymore. Relationships aren't one-sided. They don't start without just cause. No one stays in a hopeless relationship when they can leave. The only reason mom was able to play bad cop all those years was because dad let her.

The friend who married the soldier from the bus lost him to a shooting accident a year after their marriage. Not long after, she went shopping for an answering machine so she wouldn't have to answer her phone calls anymore. But whenever I called, she picked up before the third ring. She was the one who'd told me about the dove complex.

"Female doves are devoted to their mates, but they die young. They grow

30

sick from giving so much love and never receiving any. It's the same with people. Everyone wants to receive as much love as they give. If you only receive love without giving any in return, you're slowly killing the other person. Aren't relationships frightening?"

Last time I checked, she was still single. But I assume she'll end up with either the phone repair guy or her shrink.

I gulped down my drink, which Kang quickly refilled. Staring at the beer foam slowly make its way up to the rim, I tried to change the subject. "What is it you like about India?"

Kang turned serious. "I like its respect for diversity. It's so free."

"But if everyone wants to be free and do what they want, it'll lead to problems, like when two women start fighting over one man."

"In India, no one cares what the other person does. They respect everyone else's freedom, and let karma sort things out. Let's say someone does what he wants to do and that leads to a bad outcome. That bad karma will come back to him in the end. That's why people simply don't care."

I muttered to myself, *Does that mean mom should let the other woman have dad? Does that mean I should steal from my mom's share of happiness?*

"Even beggars think that way," Kang was continuing. "They're very arrogant, even as they're asking for change. They're not grateful to the person who gives them money. Instead, they think the other person should be grateful to them for giving them the opportunity to do a good deed."

Park, who prides himself on taking a balanced outlook on everything, offered a new interpretation.

"Maybe that's because the population is so poor. Two percent of Indians have all the wealth, while the other ninety-eight percent have nothing. Because they have nothing, they're free. This one friend of mine, a travel agent, invited an Indian tour guide to Korea once…"

It didn't seem like the stories of India were going to end. I kept drinking. Later, I didn't wait for Kang to top me off, opting to pour the beer myself.

"Anyway, this tour guide used to be a college professor in India, an intellectual elite, but when he rode a Korean train for the first time, his eyes widened in shock. He was surprised by the power of money and order. Taiwan, Japan, and Korea are the safest countries in the world, but Korea outdoes the others in standards and control."

Kang shouted, "Look, the Indians are fine with what they have. Why would they need order?"

Park, who considers himself a born leader, insisted, "I'm saying they're different from Koreans, because we can't live without material possessions. We can't live the kind of life Indians have." Then, as with all other talkative bossy types who believe themselves to be anti-establishment, Park suddenly yelled, "Now, let's rid ourselves of obsession! Let's shed all earthly ties!" Then lifting his glass, he proposed, or rather, demanded, a toast.

I turned to Kang. I felt my tongue go dry. "Remember the frame that was hanging on the classroom wall where you used to teach? What was written on it?"

"'The truth shall set you free.' I finally understand the meaning of that. We're supposed to get rid of all our possessions. That, and love our neighbors. Then we'll be free. And virtuous. That's what it meant." Kang once again brought his hand to my shoulder. "Seeing as how you're craving freedom, you must be getting tired of this life as well." After shaking his head a few times, he drew near, and with beer on his breath, grabbed my shoulders. "Come with me to Calcutta. And let's never return." He was squeezing me a little too hard for my liking, but I was too drunk to put up a fight.

Solitude had long been my companion. At times, I turned to alcohol, which helped me pretend I wasn't lonely. I had skill as a designer, which earned me rent and enough money to put away in savings. I had a solid doodling habit. I had a full head of hair, which I could cut or grow out as much as I pleased. I had plenty of years before me, enough to move to several new places and then some. I could take up studying English, as well as continue learning French. I could spend the rest of my life sitting at a park bench in Calcutta, sharing my morning breakfast roll with the park's huge rats as we chase away the crows. I could even get married. I possessed so many things, including things I didn't need. Like freedom. And attachment.

The young owner of the bar came over and told us they were ready to close. Just then, a man and a woman walked in. The woman looked to be in her twenties. The man was at least twice her age. The owner told them business hours were over. The man didn't want to leave. The girl looked even more upset. "Can we just have one bottle of beer before we go?"

Annoyed, the owner shot back, "Look, I told you. Business hours are over!" He obviously thought little of her. At that, I shot up from my seat. I screamed, "Hey! You!"

The owner was about to turn and face me when suddenly, he let out a wail and fell to the floor. Someone from another table had thrown an empty bottle across the bar. A woman ran, screaming. This was followed by shouts and the sound of glass breaking. Two men who were sitting at the bar ran to the table. They'd come separately, but, upon discovering they were both wearing ROTC rings, became fast friends and decided to sit together. But not even these ex-army guys could break up the fight. In fact, it only grew worse. Someone flew across the room and fell on our table, dragging us into the brawl. The men, the owner, and my own colleagues started throwing punches. It was dark inside, like the stage of a theater.

People were flying left and right, and falling into broken glass and pools of beer. Coming to his senses, Kang pushed me toward the front door. The shock sent my glasses flying to the floor. I heard my glasses crunch underneath someone's shoe, the same way those chips did when my dad stomped on them all those years ago.

Everyone had blood on their shirts, even if it didn't belong to them. Buttons had long since gone missing. Some had torn sleeves. One customer had to be rushed to a nearby hospital ER where he suffered eleven stitches on his forehead without any anesthetic because hospitals don't administer anesthetic to drunk patients. The only people who managed to escape unscathed that night were the old man and his younger lover.

Later, Kang told me, "That fight started because of you. Everyone was drunk and not thinking straight. That's when you started shouting. Why'd you do that? And why did you throw the bottle at that girl who was leaving? It's a good thing it hit the door. If you'd hit her, her sugar daddy would have done something. Where'd you go that night, anyway? You didn't even stop for an umbrella."

That night, I ran outside and into the rain. Kang called after me, but all I could hear was my phone ringing at home, my mom desperately trying to reach me.

The next day, I found myself sitting at the hotel bar with a bad cough. Han was angry.

"I never liked that Kang. I don't like the way he talks. I hate his ponytail and those jeans he wears. He's full of shit. Does he think he's an expert on India now? I don't want you drinking with him again," he growled as he rubbed out a Dunhill. Wrinkles furrowed his forehead. "How long have you known him anyway?"

When I was in high school, there was a guy who always sat behind me on the bus. Once, he followed me home and told me my ankles were pretty.

"Who's that boy?" my dad had asked, frowning.

That night, Han slept in my apartment.

I told myself that would be our last night together. I didn't sleep.

Me

My birthday fell in the fourth week of October. After Kang returned from India, we got more work, so I had to work late the night of my birthday. Han waited for me at the bar in the lower level.

"Don't wait for me. I might have to work all night," I informed him.

"I can wait all night," he'd quickly replied.

He knew I was trying to avoid him. He sat there for three hours, enduring the loud pop music handpicked by the bar owner/aspiring singer, and the uproarious laughter of the insurance saleswomen who were sitting at a nearby table. He thought he could impress me by waiting.

My face was expressionless as I descended the stairs to the bar. He was sitting in one corner, in an olive suit and an eggplant tie, the same color combination I'd used on a book cover I'd just designed. He and I had a lot in common. A bitter smile came to my lips. I knew exactly what it was I was feeling. Most people would identify it as "the pain of a breakup," when, in truth, it was closer to "the unwillingness to let go."

On the table, he placed a small box with a ring inside. Then he announced he and his wife had begun sleeping in separate bedrooms. He thought this was sure to be a great birthday gift. When I pushed the box back toward him, he sat motionless, his eyes trained on me. I don't know how long we stayed that way.

Later, I found myself standing alone outside, waiting for the lights to change so I could cross the street. Nearby were a clothing shop, a stationery store, and a bakery—all closed. A few neon signs were the only light. The wind swept back my long hair. At least I had my mom's thick hair—that much was true. A leaf fell and landed near my feet. I was born in the most depressing of weathers. The light finally changed. I became lost in the crowd; my footsteps picked up speed.

Passing by a hotel, I almost stepped in a pile of vomit. There was no one at the bus stop. The buses had stopped running. The small kiosk where I sometimes purchased bus tokens was gated shut. I saw a woman crouching by the sidewalk as a male companion attempted to flag down a cab. Dirty plastic clinging to a newspaper dispenser fluttered in the wind. A nearby trash can was overflowing with empty bottles and cans. One man was sobbing next to it. A passerby gave him a dull, sidelong glance before continuing on in an unbroken pace. The night wore on. Time was passing by.

Arriving home, I took off my jacket and was unzipping my skirt when the phone rang. I didn't pick up. It rang again when I was in the shower. It rang for a long time.

It rang again late that night. Turning in my bed, I reached for the phone.

"I can't sleep. Yesterday, I had a hard time doing your father's laundry. I was taking his underwear and shirts out of the water when they gave off a horrible smell. The stink was so bad I couldn't bear it. We lived together a long time, your father and I, but even after all these years, we're still strangers. That's not how it is with my children. One doesn't grow to hate her kids because of something they did. These days, I'm reminded of what my late mother told me. During the war, the soldiers who told their mothers where they were hiding survived, but the ones who told their wives were discovered and killed. One summer, my father fell asleep on a cold slab of rock and he woke up with his mouth turned sideways. My mother couldn't bear to look at him. She actually considered leaving him, but fortunately, acupuncture brought his mouth back to where it should be. That was the end of that."

In my groggy state, I remembered that I hadn't stopped by the bank that day. I had to pay my bills and put money in my savings account, but more than that, I had to give my dad his money back. I was about to ask Mom for her bank account number but I stopped. My relationship with her will still be there when I wake up tomorrow. I can ask her then. This time, I wouldn't have to worry about getting my period while at the bank. Changing the rules isn't such a bad thing. It wasn't so bad to enjoy a break from solitude.

I turned to look at the window, where the morning sun was already rising. A new day. I'm my father's daughter. I'm just like him. I'm my father's woman. I'm my mother's daughter. I'm her rival. I'm his woman. I'm his wife's rival. I'm just like his wife. And I'm me. I'm me.

All this happened three years ago.

Time goes on. No. Time stands still. I'm the one passing by, just like the morning crowd hurrying down the streets every day without stopping to wonder about the many faceless rooms inside the buildings.

The important thing is to not look back.

35

Bruise

I

Mail arrived over the weekend. One piece was in an envelope with a plastic window over where the recipient's name and address were printed. Two were in plain white envelopes. One was in a thick manila folder with a dozen stamps arranged in two rows on the top right corner.

In the age of email, where regular mail is so rare, it's easy to tell the contents of your mail by the envelope. One of the white envelopes was from Hansung Culture Foundation. I guessed it was an invitation to an awards ceremony for a writing contest for which I was a guest judge. One was from the BC Credit Card Company. Obviously, my credit card bill. I could probably guess the amount due. This month, I'd bought a white gold necklace for my wife on our wedding anniversary. Also this month, some of my friends had dragged me to a hostess bar. I'd filled up my car three times this month. I also had a couple meals at the Japanese restaurant near the college where I teach. The last payment for the new 500-liter refrigerator I'd bought my mother was also due this month.

The remaining envelope was stamped with the logo for I-Sense Eyewear, next to a drawing of an owl. It was thick and stiff. It must be I-Sense Eyewear wishing me a happy wedding anniversary, the way it probably does to every customer on its mailing list.

The manila folder was a mystery. Judging from the neat handwriting spelling "Professor Lee Jin-chan, Department of Korean Education" and "Kang-dong, Jugong APT 303-208," the sender was female. But her name—Han Hyun—didn't ring a bell.

I unlocked the door to my office and tossed the mail on my desk. As always, I put my bag down, hung my jacket up, and turned on the computer. With practiced motions, I turned on the heater and poured water into the electric kettle.

The chair creaked when I sat on it. Leaning back, I took a look around the office. Almost by instinct, my gaze shifted to what lay outside the window, like a tropical fish trapped in a tank sticking its head out for a gasp of air. What I thought would be a short intake of breath came out as a weary sigh. I hadn't planned on the sigh, but it, too, was part of my morning routine.

Another day began.

I took a lens cleaner from one of the drawers and proceeded to wipe my glasses. Putting the cleaner back, my hand brushed against the pure chill of a stainless steel letter opener. I'd bought it at a souvenir shop after touring the Mayan Inca Exhibition. Slowly, I slid the letter opener across the manila folder. The electric kettle was making angry noises, as if resisting what was about to come. Inevitably though, the water began to boil. The flap on the thick folder also resisted before giving way.

There were no surprises. Inside was a stack of typed manuscript pages. On the cover page were the words *Traces of Bruising* in a fifteen-point bold font. It looked to be fiction. Given my work as a freelance columnist and "literary critic" in several newspapers, I sometimes received these sorts of things in the mail. *Traces of Bruising*. The title was as unremarkable as the author's name. The novel began with a quote from a poem—never a powerful introduction.

If, by leaving the orbit, it meant I could never enter it again. . .

I was settling down to read the piece when a sudden, sharp ping pierced the air. It came from my computer, which had been peacefully slumbering in screensaver mode.

Tucking the manuscript back into the manila folder, I pulled myself to the desk.

When the school board announced it was endowing all the teaching staff with an internet connection, the decision wasn't construed as agenda-free; after all, this was a board that made everything about money. Our fears were proven correct. Several times a day, this dreaded ping drew meek, helpless professors to their computer screens like so many remote-controlled robots, where pop-up notices commanded them variously to teach students to value school property, set an example in greeting the deans with respect, reduce use of the elevators, conserve water, etc. These notices unfailingly ended with the postscript *We kindly ask for your cooperation*, which was no less alarming than having burly, tattooed thugs cornering you in a street alley. No longer could the staff make excuses about not having received the notice in the mail or getting the telephone call.

At a recent work dinner, one colleague complained that the school felt more like an army than a school.

To this, another colleague, who'd been an army drill sergeant in a former life remarked, "No army does what this school does. Juvenile detention centers, maybe."

I remember reading somewhere that juvenile detention centers were the worst of both worlds—school and prison.

"This is how organizations are. There's nothing we can do," another professor had bleated weakly, signaling the close of the conversation.

Back at my desk, I pressed the ENTER key to dissolve the screensaver and reveal the pop-up sent from the academic affairs office. It told us to recommend to students that they participate in tomorrow's open class. It went on to "kindly ask" for our participation as well. This was the third notice about the open class in two days. Administrators clearly wanted to milk this lecture and its $120-an-hour speaker for all it was worth. The speaker was famed novelist Park Chung, whose talk was titled, "Literature and Life." When I called a few days ago, Chung seemed pleased to hear my voice.

"We're the only ones from our college class still in the writing business. Would it kill you to call more often?" he complained good-humoredly.

"Believe me, I wish I didn't know you. I only call when I need a favor," I countered, keeping up the banter. I wasn't a subscriber to the idea that you had to befriend someone just because they were from the same hometown or the same school. The belief stayed no less firm even when Chung obliged my requests to speak to my class. ("Can you come speak to my kids again?" "Depends. How much do I get? Is it enough beers to get you good and drunk?")

I stirred two teaspoons of instant decaf coffee into a mug of hot water.

Outside, the sky was gray. Far away were some streets, across which lay several blocks of apartment buildings covered in a haze. In one of those apartments was my wife, probably retching from the rice soup she'd forced herself to eat. Our five-year-old daughter would be frowning in concentration as she worked on a grammar book, placing stickers in their appropriate boxes.

As I was leaving the house that morning, my wife had announced, "I'm going to the doctor today."

I didn't say anything. She practically spat those words at me. I thought *doctor* meant the shrink she saw last year for her insomnia. Now I realized she might have been talking about her ob-gyn. This latest bout of depression began when we failed at contraception.

When my wife was six months pregnant with our daughter, she underwent surgery to remove a lump from her uterus. It was growing at a speed comparable to the fetus and was posing a real threat to our unborn baby. We had no choice but to opt for the surgery. It was done anesthesia-free for the sake of our daughter's health. After the surgery, my wife took to scoffing at any woman who complained of the pains of childbirth.

"All pain is designed to be bearable. Those women are complaining about nothing. I was completely conscious when doctors slashed my belly, went in, dug around, found the lump, and cut it out. I survived, but no one can possibly imagine that kind of pain." She'd then stare blankly at moms on TV who drew their children close for hugs and kisses.

That was around the same time I got the job at the community college, and my wife and I left Seoul for the suburbs. It was a difficult transition for her since she'd lived in the city all her life and shared the same zip code with her mother even after we were married, a coincidence that my mother-in-law interpreted as a request for help and interference. In the suburbs, my wife was left to raise our child completely on her own. Being a weak woman, the strains of child-rearing and housework were too much to bear. They didn't come easily to her like they did to some women. Even during those precious hours the baby slept, she didn't sleep. She was too busy mourning her life.

Except for the telephone, I was her only source of comfort. She wanted to spend time with me, a desire that depended on two conditions: the baby had to be sleeping, and I had to not be tired. Neither was easily met. I was always exhausted. In exchange for the professorship, I had to make certain contributions or donations to the school; failing that, I had to forfeit a per centage of my monthly wages to the school toward its "growth and development." Given this administrative pressure, it wasn't easy to focus on teaching, especially when the students were largely unmotivated. Moreover, I was terrified I might not finish my dissertation before my self-imposed deadline of the beginning of next semester, because I was exhausted from dealing with administrative chores and campus politics. Often, my brother called to try and persuade me to take out more bank loans for him with my "solid credit as a successful professor," and when I refused, my mother called to demand why I was being so heartless and turning my back on my own brother "as if it would kill me to be more considerate of his suffering." How was she supposed to face my father in the afterlife with the way her sons were behaving?

Around that time, my wife declared that the only way she could get the minimum amount of sleep required for survival was if I took care of the baby at least two nights a week. Despite the ultimatum, I always went to bed before she did. Sometimes, I woke up in the middle of the night to help with the diaper-changing or the formula-mixing, but I had too many problems of my own to make that a regular habit.

The only thing that sustained my wife through those years was the anticipation that our daughter would soon turn four years old. She was set on finding a job once the baby was old enough for kindergarten. When we married, she quit the pharmacy job she'd held for six years at a general hospital, announcing she'd had enough of work. Now, she wanted to open her own pharmacy. Because we didn't have the money for it, however, she had to find a salaried job again. She thought she'd find part-time work. She began making calls to her friends still in the practice, but the search didn't go well. I found her sitting in front of the mirror, frowning at her lower belly. Sometimes, she'd sigh deeply as she rubbed moisturizer on her face. She also took to gossiping, nastily, about the neighbors. One kid from the playground was unnaturally short for his age, she told me, guessing that his working mom was too busy to pay the poor kid any attention. She experienced wild mood swings. Sometimes, she seemed weak and listless. Other times, she became intensely aggressive. We got into more fights than when she was pregnant. She never admitted out loud that she wanted her own pharmacy. She expressed her frustration in other ways, like complaining that I scattered cigarette ash everywhere or left the newspaper on the toilet bowl lid.

She took up bowling. She even signed up for lessons on how to play the small bamboo flute. But none of these eclectic hobbies enriched her life, the way some of the advertising leaflets promised. When a neighbor gave her a rosewood rosary she'd bought on a pilgrimage to the Vatican, she accompanied her to church a few times but failed at finding inner peace. My wife was growing unhappier; at least when the baby was a newborn, her own issues could be put on the back burner. Now, she was tormented by the fact that she had no one, including me, to blame for her unhappiness.

Two weeks ago, she realized she'd missed her period. Finally, she had something real to direct her anger at.

She never wanted a second child. And I certainly didn't want her to repeat the misery she suffered the first time around. The solution seemed obvious. But my wife didn't run to the ob-gyn. Instead, she seethed. She'd finally found something to hate, and it lay growing inside her. Meanwhile, her blood vessels were succumbing to pressure and soon, the capillaries near the surface of her skin burst. They took the shape of many little bruises.

Traces of bruising.

My gaze shifted back to my desk. The yellow manila folder lay where I'd put it. My coffee had gone cold. I lifted the mug. I'd gotten into the habit of drinking cold coffee early in the morning, when I didn't have to expect company.

Bringing the cup to my lips, my eyes suddenly widened in delayed realization. That name—Han Hyun—finally struck a chord in my memory.

2

That night, Chung and I sat before steaming cups of *sake* with dried strips of fish scales delicately floating on top.

Chung blew on the cup before slowly bringing it to his lips. With his head slightly lowered, I had a better view of the gray hairs that had sprouted along his center part. Every time he crinkled his forehead, fine wrinkles formed around his eyes. Because he was the oldest son in a family full of children, Chung had always projected a mature aura, even in college. We still had a couple of years left before we turned forty, but he already more than looked the part. I knew I didn't look much different. It's just that I was used to constantly seeing myself, so the shock had lost its edge.

Seeing an old friend again after a long hiatus is the single best way to alert you to how much you've aged. It's as if confronting the changed contours of a friend's face last seen ten years ago adds ten years to your own life. After twenty years, the revelation is even more poignant. The heavy remorse of the past twenty years comes at you like a brick hurled at full speed.

My wife had said something similar not long ago. She'd run into a college friend at a grocery store, who updated her on the status of their mutual friends.

"You remember Mi-kyung, don't you?" her friend had asked excitedly. "She lives in our apartment building. Her husband has his own dentistry practice."

"Already? How old is he?" my wife had exclaimed.

"I don't know. Maybe forty?"

"Forty?" my wife gaped. Without thinking, she blurted, "Why'd she marry a guy so much older?"

Telling me this story, my wife had smiled ruefully. "I forgot that next year, you'll be forty. And I'll be thirty-six. I was so caught up with my day-to-day life that I didn't realize my life was passing me by."

"Time has really passed," Chung was saying as he reached for a piece of sashimi. "We used to drink cheap soju with kimchi in college, and now look at us! We're sitting here with sake and sashimi. In this bad economy!" He burst out laughing.

"You know," he continued, "I was at another Japanese place a few days ago. I have a friend from middle school who owns a string of successful auto repair shops. He's always trying to buy me drinks. You know how writers are in real life. We don't always sit in our nooks and write serious fiction all day, Hemingway-like. We write bulletins and columns and go on speaking engagements and judge women's magazine essays. But when I tell my friend I'm busy, he imagines I'm on a trip seeking inspiration for my magnum opus or schmoozing with friends. When a magazine or newspaper prints an interview with me, he gets it laminated and hangs it in his shop. He brags to his customers that we're best friends. When they hear that, the customers show him more respect, calling him 'sir.' Can you believe that?"

With his chopsticks, he lifted several stems of roasted enoki mushrooms. He continued, "Every time I write a new book, he somehow hears about it and calls me. He tells me he buys ten copies and hands them out as gifts to customers. He says he admires me for churning out three books a year."

Chung tossed back the sake, which had now cooled. "I write a novel every time there's an event in my life. I wrote one when my wife had our baby. I

42

wrote one when my brother went to college. How many masterpieces is that? Am I some kind of genius?"

I gulped down my drink and scoffed, "You have to be unrecognized in your own time to be a certified genius, which usually happens to people who die young. You're already forty. You're too old to die young now."

"You're right," Chung grinned. "Now that I'm old, all I can do is live out my days until my time comes."

Our conversation shifted to news about our friends. Chung was usually the messenger in this.

One guy we both knew had left his job at an advertising firm to start an *udon* restaurant. He was living a simple life making around $400 a day, before his back gave out, leaving him crippled. Another guy left his teaching job after joining a leftist teachers' union. His wife became the family breadwinner, selling insurance until she began an affair and left her husband. One other friend built a six-story parking ramp on some expensive real estate his father had given him, but he ran into problems when he couldn't obtain the correct permits. One girl we both knew had worked as a TV writer before marrying a musician's manager and divorcing him after a few months. The prettiest, smartest, and snobbiest girl from our department had gone to the U.S. with her husband, where they were running a dry cleaning business. One friend read in a magazine that Chung lived nearby and solicited him to subscribe to a book series before breaking down in tears and begging him to take a look at his manuscript.

Chung sighed, "That's life. Dreams disappear, journeys become too long."

Downing three cups of hot *sake* had left me with a headache. Chung's story of the soliciting friend made me debate whether or not to tell him about Hyun.

Surprisingly, it was Chung who brought her up. Lighting a cigarette, he took a deep drag and croaked, "Did you hear about Young?"

"Shim Young? I heard he works at a publishing house somewhere. I think he may have debuted as a poet, although I've yet to read one of his works."

"He's no poet. He lied about writing poetry to impress Hyun," Chung spat. His voice shook imperceptibly when he said her name.

At one point, Chung, Hyun, and I had been on campus at the same time. I'd finished my stint as an army officer and was newly enrolled in a Ph.D program. Chung had also come back from the army and was a senior. Hyun was a sophomore, I think. Shim Young was also on campus then. He'd been expelled as a freshman for participating in a student riot but had gotten himself readmitted. He and I were both on campus for only one semester, so I didn't know him that well.

I knew very little about Hyun. When I saw her, she was always with Chung. They were in the same literary society. I remember having lunch with them in the cafeteria a few times. Young may have been there, too. She gave the impression of a sweet young girl, as cared for and pampered as a prize orchid. She looked prim and neat even when eating Chinese black bean noodles. I wasn't shocked when she left school to marry Young after finding out she was four months pregnant. She seemed naïve and old-fashioned in that way some people are who are desperate to control their lives. That was the extent of my knowledge of her. I never had a huge interest in gossip.

After two more puffs, Chung rubbed out his cigarette and continued.

"About a month ago, Young got into a huge car accident."

"How?" I asked.

"You really didn't know what he was doing with his life, did you? 'How?' You're the first person to ask that. Most people's reactions have been, 'I'm not surprised.'"

Chung didn't mask his contempt. He continued, "Young's been going around having fun while his wife stayed home with their child. I don't know if he had a job or if he went around mooching drinks off people. He promised me that big things were coming his way, that he was starting a new business. I guess he never came to see you."

"We weren't close."

"I wasn't close to him, either! But I don't think that mattered to him. We're talking about a forty-year-old guy who gets wasted and passes out on the sidewalk."

A few years ago, Chung saw him at a taxi stop near Sinchon station. It was past midnight. Chung, on his way home, was trying to get a cab when he saw a man completely drunk and sprawled out on the curb. Two cab drivers were trying to shake him awake. Half his body was draped across the sidewalk, with his head leaning out into the street. No amount of shaking could force him awake. Exasperated, the drivers practically kicked him back to the sidewalk. When he rolled over, Chung got a look at the man's face. It was Young, wearing a tattered suit covered in spit and dirt.

The next morning, Young woke up in Chung's house. Chung's wife made him hot stew with bean sprouts. Young didn't show any inclination to leave, even after breakfast.

"Don't you have to go to work?" Chung had asked.

"Nah, they'll only yell at me again," he yawned.

"Shouldn't you, um, call home?" Chung asked awkwardly, thinking of the woman who must be waiting for him.

"No need," he replied shortly.

Chung was scheduled to speak as a guest on a radio program on fiction writing that morning. Young still didn't make any signs to leave. Instead, he walked Chung to the front door and, with Chung's young son, waved good-bye. When Chung returned that afternoon, Young was passed out drunk next to his desk and a bottle of *soju*. Chung's wife was none too pleased and took it out on her husband as soon as the *persona non grata* finally left. According to Chung, women have the uncanny ability to not only blame men for what they're fighting about but also dredge up similar grudges they can link to the current argument.

Young constantly called Chung after that. Chung listened patiently, alternating between contempt and pity as Young spoke grandiosely about his passion for literature and his business plans. Chung offered his home to Young, bought him drinks, and even lent him money that was never returned. Chung didn't realize his friendship would be extorted for such a long time. Once, Chung heard the frenzied barking of stray dogs in the street. Running out, he found Young passed out over a pile of his own vomit. Another time, he wet Chung's bed. One night, he told a woman he met at a bar that he was good friends with a popular novelist, who'd "love to have them over for more drinks." When they banged on his door and rang the doorbell late that night, even Chung, who'd been called a saint more than once by people who knew the situation, finally reached his limit.

We were in our early twenties when Young was expelled from college. When he participated in the protest and was dragged off by the riot police, we had heavy, sinking feelings of guilt. There he was, a real activist, while the rest of us stayed safe and sound in our homes. To students of that time, Young was a debt we owed, a tab he could collect any time he wished. Chung, who was class president then, suffered the strongest pangs of conscience. But perhaps losing Hyun was enough penance— or perhaps not.

"On the day of the accident, he was completely hammered," Chung was saying. "Apparently, he showed up at the awards ceremony for the Yongin

Book Awards. The winner was a former professor at our school who'd retired before we arrived on campus, so Young couldn't have known the guy at all. I don't know why he went. A friend of mine who was there told me that Young went with them to the bars afterward, whooping and cheering."

His friend hadn't recognized Young until he approached and introduced himself. "You're a writer, aren't you? I'm Shim Young, class of '79."

The friend replied, "Ah, then you must know Park Chung." That was a mistake. Guilty by association, this friend had to suffer Young all night. When they went out for drinks, Young downed his alcohol in a hurry. He talked incessantly, slurring his words. Most of his talk was lewd and inappropriate. The friend felt a strong desire to let people know they weren't friends. When Young went to the bathroom, he scurried to another seat. By that time, most people were cheerfully drunk and mingling. Someone else sat in the empty chair next to Young, but he, too, soon left. Young began dancing. He tried to embrace some of the female writers and pull them close, a maneuver they resisted fiercely. Humiliated, he started sniffling.

The friend had gone to the table where the winner sat. Someone pointed to Young and asked the honored poet, "Was he one of your students? I heard he went to your university."

"No, I've never seen him before," the poet replied.

"So what's he doing here? And why is he behaving like that?"

The poet smiled generously and answered, "Leave him be. It happens at parties when everyone's had a little too much alcohol and a little too much excitement." Then softly, he murmured, "After all, parties have always been magnets for strays and beggars."

"Can you imagine that? He stayed until the end and begged everyone to stay for one last drink. Of course he got into an accident!" Chung shook his head.

"Did you visit him at the hospital?"

"I thought about it but decided not to. I got the news late, and besides, I don't want to see Hyun reduced to..."

Chung sipped a mouthful of the seafood soup that had gone cold. He started coughing from the chili peppers.

"Now that college was so long ago, I can say what I really think," Chung sputtered, "I don't think Young was a genuine supporter of those riots. I mean, he was only handing out leaflets! He was just in the wrong place at the wrong time."

He looked bitter as he reached for a glass of water.

"His entire life is one big show," he continued. "He has absolutely no responsibility. Do you know how he got his job? Remember Kim Bum-su, the guy who asked him to hand out those leaflets? Bum-su started a publishing company after he got out of jail. When he heard about Young, he gave him a job writing company bulletins. At first, Young must have done a good job. Bum-su thought he was creative and fresh. But the problem was he wasn't accountable. He'd take all the materials and promise to get the work done, then disappear for days. Apparently, Bum-su lost a couple big clients that way. Young kept playing that same trick—all talk, no follow through. But whenever they went out for drinks, he was a hit with the ladies. They thought he had a pure soul."

Chung continued, "He drank away the money his wife had saved to pay for the birth of their baby. Hyun had to borrow more money before she went to the hospital to have the child. Young showed up drunk the day after she gave birth and got into a fight with a hospital security guard. Hyun had to beg and plead to make him leave. I still don't understand what she saw in him. She's not dumb enough to fall for hot air."

I glimpsed at the clock on the wall. It read eleven o'clock. I changed the subject.

"How are your wife and kids?"

"Oh, the same. Our younger kid is starting grade school this year. Grade school, not elementary school. When I write 'elementary school,' my publisher always changes it. Now I catch myself saying grade school. It's like having my own autocorrect, you know, the function on your word processing that goes ping! and automatically corrects the spelling or grammar mistakes you've deliberately included in your writing. Like putting a space between 'stop' and 'light.' Later, I find myself steering away from using those words altogether. I don't know what you'd call that. Maybe rebellion?"

"At our age? Hardly. Maybe adaptation? Or maybe you're just giving up."

It was getting late and we were getting drunk. Our conversation trailed off. Chung became noticeably quiet. I thought back to Hyun's manuscript, lying in a drawer in my darkened office. Why'd she send the manuscript to me and not Chung?

It was only a ten-minute walk to the campus from the bar. I briefly considered going to get the manuscript and giving it to Chung. I had an idea what her story might be about and wasn't sure I could be a sympathetic reader to a woman spilling out her woes on paper. It would probably be better for everyone involved to bring in someone who actually cared. I glanced at Chung. He was lost in his own thoughts. We ordered one last round.

Nursing his drink, Chung murmured, "It would have ended the same way."

I sipped the hot *sake* and waited for him to continue.

"Even if Hyun had married me, not Chung, our life would have been the same. We'd fight and argue, and feel sorry for one another as we grew older. She'd have gone through the same ordeals and trials I'm putting my wife through. I shudder to think of her nagging me the way my wife does. Maybe it was a good thing he stole her from me."

Silently, he looked down at the liquid swirling in his cup. His wide-eyed expression was reflected back to him. Smiling sadly, he slowly took another sip. His cheeks were red.

"But you know..." he whispered, "I still think I would have liked to have shared a life with her. I don't think that feeling will ever go away."

"Maybe that's like a bruise."

"Bruise?"

Ignoring the question, I asked him about the accident. "When did Young leave the hospital?"

"I heard he had surgery but don't know what happened after that. Maybe he's home now. Why? Are you thinking of visiting him?"

"No."

One of the servers appeared, asking and if she could clear our table.

"Would you like your bill now?" she asked me, as I was the regular customer.

When he saw me take out my credit card, Chung reached for his own. I waved him away and handed the server my card.

"It's just... the bruising," I said, rather inexplicably.

"Why all this talk about bruises?"

"I received a manuscript from a woman, and it had that word in the title."

"Who is she?"

"She's... just someone."

Losing interest, Chung nodded and put on his jacket.

Outside, the night air felt cold. Some of the signboards were still flickering, but the streets were eerily silent.

"How will you get to Seoul at this hour? Stay the night at my place," I offered, but Chung insisted that he could catch a cab to Sillim station, from where he could take one of the night buses home.

"We're not close enough to be sleepover buddies, are we? Call me again when you need me," he laughed good-humoredly. Even in the dark, I could see the shadows cast on his face by his wrinkles.

A taxi came to a stop. Chung climbed in, pulling his old bag in after him. The cab didn't leave right away. They were probably haggling the price. Somewhat embarrassed, I crossed the street at the next light. Reaching the other side, I looked back and saw Chung getting out of the cab. Waving, he ran to another taxi. His trench coat flapped immodestly at the knee. His bag was tucked under one arm, with his hand buried in his pocket. His fingers were probably brushing against the envelope he'd received that day containing his speaking fee. It was only November but the night air was utterly cold.

3

Several days later, I finally got around to reading Hyun's manuscript.

That morning as I was getting ready to leave, my wife was standing by our doorway, waiting.

"I should really see a doctor today," she'd announced, looking to me for a response.

I assumed she meant her ob-gyn, and that she'd already come to a decision, so I didn't say anything. Even if common-sense dictated that decisions should be made mutually, when I thought of the pain my wife went through with our daughter, I believed she had the right to call the shots about what goes on with her body.

The sky was still gray. There were many gray days this winter. The air felt thick and close. It didn't smell like it'd snow anytime soon. After emailing the questions I was to use for my students' midterms, I turned to gaze out the window. I picked up the manuscript, not thinking much about it.

Traces of Bruising

If, by leaving the orbit, it meant I could never enter it again, at least I'll know that the comet that flew across the sky was free—that freedom only comes to those who give up.

—From Kim Joong's "Breaking Orbit"

He's gone. He's on a trip.

He always wanted to leave, so I'm sure he's happy now, wherever he is. He'd always felt suffocated here, like a circus giant folded into a tiny box and moaning from the exertion. Wherever he is now, he must be happier there. Even so, I'm waiting for him to return. When he does, I'll buy him tubes of paint. Did he want paint? I don't know. But he'd need something— paint, a tree, a rock—that he can call his own. Is it too late? No matter. I can wait forever.

A few days ago, he came home drunk. Again. He never rings the door- bell, preferring to kick the door instead. He's the only man I've ever heard of who yells "Anyone there?" while wildly kicking at his own front door. When I opened the door, he fell on top of me like a stiff corpse hidden in a closet falling upon its discoverer. With practiced patience, I dragged him to the living room and to the sofa.

Even as his body lay crumpled, he held his head high. When drunk, his head never bent down. I've tried pressing down on it, even going so far as to climb on his stomach, dig my knees into his shoulders, and push his head as hard as I could. His eyes remained closed, like a dead man's, but his head never budged. And when I tried to remove his shoes, he kicked me. I had no choice but to leave him as he was, his head awkwardly tilted, the rest of his body limp.

On days he came home drunk, I'd set the alarm for six a.m. so I could wake him and coax him into our bedroom before our daughter awakened and saw him. My rule was to never hide our problems from our daughter, such as our struggle to pay the bills. But a drunk father was different. She was too young to understand the changes her father was going through.

Once, she woke up before I did. When I wandered out to the living room, I found her staring down at her wasted father.

"Mom, why's dad sleeping with his shoes on?" She asked.

"I don't know. He must have somewhere he wants to go."

"In his sleep?" she asked. Slowly, she removed his shoes, murmuring, "He must be tired from walking all night."

The next morning, waking up in our bed, I immediately thought of how uncomfortable his sleep must have been in that awkward position. Did he sleep okay? I hastened to bring him to bed so his neck wouldn't be as stiff anymore.

I approached him and took off his clothes. His skin had the faint yellowish markings of days-old bruises. He tripped and fell often and frequently got lost. And the more he did, the more threadbare his suits became, and the longer the bruises stayed on his body. Bruises remain sore to the touch until they turn a sickly green color, after which they cease to hurt at all. By the time they turn yellow, he'd be hard pressed to remember where he got them in the first place. The initial bump that got him the bruise would have faded into distant memory. And soon, he'd come home with fresh bruises.

Now, as I wipe down his body with a warm wet cloth, I study the folds of his skin, the changes in the setting and angles of his bones. He's changed so much during the ten-odd years we've been together. His once-thick dark brown hair has thinned. His forehead is readying itself for imminent baldness. The lines on his body have become erratic from his stooped shoulders and bloated stomach.

Aging is a process that occurs to everyone; time doesn't stand still for others while one person ages. My husband's body seems to be doing what everyone else's is doing. I only wish his life would follow an ordinary trajectory as well.

He was born in April, 1959. His mother married into a family where children were rare and promptly birthed six sons, one after the other. Proud of her achievement, she lifted her spoon high when she ate her meals. His father was a prosperous farmer in a small village down south. His six sons never knew the meaning of poverty. The sons were of differing breeds; one was tall, one was short, one fat, one skinny. Their father was well versed in philosophers like Laozi and Zhuangzi and fittingly, the sons behaved well and stayed in line. The youngest child was sometimes late, coming home after dark, and grew easily bored, but even this was an admissible trait, a small peculiarity given the number of children.

This youngest child grew up free, with nothing holding him back. Aside from taking a year off school when he was twelve years old due to a sudden sickness, he had a normal childhood.

51

Nothing much changed in his teenage years. He found school a little stuffy, but he coped by copying Kim Soo-young's poems into his notebook and singing along to rock music in his room. He had almost no friends, which meant his school life was fairly monotonous. His grades were average, and earned him a quiet, unremarkable entry into college. He took nothing too seriously. He had no obsessions. He didn't fret over things like friends or grades. Nothing restricted his child-like, childish sensibilities. Until…

He was just a freshman when he was expelled, making him, at twenty-two, a high school dropout. He had no skill set, so jobs were hard to come by. He tried to find work at a small manufacturing company run by a relative but was discouraged by the concern that it'd look like he got in through the back door. In the end, he got a job at a small publisher's. At first, he worked as a cutter then moved on to etching, finally getting promoted to making small illustrated cuts. After months working as a trainee, he finally got his first real paycheck, part of which he promptly spent on a hooker. Leaving the red light district, he wandered out to the street. Waves of loneliness and exhaustion washed over him. Out of nowhere, he also felt a sudden will to live. He murmured, "The wind is coming. I have to keep on living." Rounding the corner at St. Peter's Church, he headed to a market. His shirt was wrinkled from his adventures with the prostitute, so he bought a new one. He was walking toward the bus stop when he suddenly saw a bus heading to the college that had kicked him out.

The bus was just starting to pull away. He began running at full speed. The bus driver saw him in the mirror, and thought briefly about stopping. But if he did, he'd have to wait thirty more seconds at the next light. So instead, the driver speeded up. But my husband didn't give up. He kept running. The driver shook his head. Finally, he stopped the bus and let the crazy young man in.

Upon getting into the bus, he felt a wave of dizziness. He'd been exerting himself all night. For a moment, he could see nothing. Gasping, he brought his hand up to his chest and willed himself to calm down. Soon, his heavy breathing subsided, with only his palm witness to the pounding of his heart. It was a little after dawn. He looked up and recognized the street he was passing. He saw his reflection, on his way to his old school. Surprised, he looked down at his unfamiliar shirt. He blushed.

When he first told me about the arrest, he grinned sheepishly. But one night, he came home drunk and fell into my arms sobbing.

"When the riot police came, I was standing there with a flag. It looked like I was waving it but I was really shivering from fear, and the shivering carried over to the flag. But I swear I didn't run. I didn't." He cried, his head and shoulders shaking, before falling asleep on my lap.

He used to say that he loved me, could sense in me a beauty as hard as the pit of a peach. He said he wanted to teach our children the music of love underneath a tree we'd plant together. He insisted that his nostrils had gotten wider after he met me, as he could finally "breathe." I married him.

Three years into our marriage, he finally finished college and got his first job, which didn't last. He came up with brilliant ideas, but felt the world was too slow in catching up to him. He was often laughed at or shunned by colleagues. His superiors didn't like his attitude. He switched jobs often, and each time he got a new one, he'd invariably get excited, start drinking, come up with interesting new plans for the job, drink some more, realize the job wasn't his calling, drown his sorrows in more drink, fall, get hurt, drink some more, skip work because he was going to be late anyway, keep missing work because he didn't want to be yelled at, drink some more, keep on drinking out of spite, then drink without being aware of what he was putting in his mouth. He took to wandering the streets at night and, along with teenage runaways, frequenting 24-hour comic book stores and arcades.

I got used to his disappearances. At first, I couldn't sleep. I called every place I could think of, as well as the police and the missing persons office. "His registration number's 590417-1480118. Yes." I waited nervously for the answer. "No reports have been made? Thank you." There were more sleepless nights than I care to mention.

Once, when he'd been gone for over a week, I called my brother-in-law. "He's never been away for this long, so..."

"Fool! When will he grow up?" His brother growled into the phone. "Listen, I'll look into this. Don't worry. Let's give him one more day."

We were still on the phone when I heard banging on the front door.

"Oh, I think that's him!"

"He's home? Tell him to stay right there. I'm on my way," he said.

An hour later, my brother-in-law came and dragged him outside. He'd obviously come to teach him a lesson. Just before he arrived, I gave my husband a bath. He waited obediently for his brother to come knocking. Putting on his shoes, he whispered, "He's going to kill me. What should I do?"

I whispered back, "It's going to be okay." I put a hand on his shoulder, but even the force of that was enough to send him toppling.

I watched them as he, with head lowered, followed his older brother out like a little kid in trouble. The autumn sunlight bounced off his back.

We were poor. I worked part-time at a small publishing house before I had our daughter. I quit after she was born, giving in to pressures from the workplace. I started accepting various editing and translating work that paid almost nothing. I wrote a fake "autobiographical" essay for a women's magazine titled "The Man Who Took My Virginity." Whenever my husband came home drunk and saw me working on those essays, he yelled, "Are you going to keep writing that bullshit? If I catch you whoring yourself like that again, I'll tear up those pages!"

The next morning, when I offered him a hastily scraped-together breakfast, he complained, "When are you getting paid for those essays? Can we have some meat for once? If you get sick or old before I do, I'm divorcing you. You hear me?"

Having a child hadn't changed anything. I'd miscarried our first baby. He was still in college at the time. Because of the trauma, it took several years before I got pregnant again. But we were just as poor as we were the first time.

Insisting that the father gets to name his children, he borrowed all sorts of idiom dictionaries and baby name lists which he pored over for days.

"My mother had a pretty name. Park Boon. It sounds pretty, and it can mean 'powder' or 'scent' in Korean. Goes either way. Or what about Bandi? Like those glittering lights? Or what about Hae? It means 'the light of the sun.' Or maybe we can name her Haemal."

Two weeks later and nearing the deadline for filing the birth certificate, I submitted the paperwork and later reported that I'd named her Jung-in.

Slapping his knee, he exclaimed, "Yes! Shim Jung-in! That's it!"

Around the time our daughter learned to sit up on her own, I was tidying up his desk when I came across a notebook I hadn't seen before. It had a thick plastic cover. He liked the smell and feel of new notebooks and pencils, but soon grew tired of them. Most of the notebooks he had were thrown away after the first few pages. Turning the page, I found that this notebook was no different.

March 19, Wednesday.
Jung-in, your daddy is going to start keeping a record of the things he's seen,

54

heard, and felt, so my time on Earth won't have been without meaning. I want you to learn about the world your father lived in. You and I are living in the same place at the same time, but your world is different from mine. Compared to your world, the world I live in is dirtier than slop, more pathetic than the front pages of a cheap tabloid. But I reassure myself in thinking that no matter how filthy history becomes—or perhaps by virtue of its filthiness—it deserves to be understood for the lessons it can bring. Tradition, no matter how dirty, is still tradition. *Jung-in*. Your mother gave you a splendid name.

March 26
Jung-in, it's been a week since I last wrote. Yesterday, I received my paycheck. Whenever they give me the envelope with the check, I get angry. An empty envelope would hold more dignity. Furious, I headed out. I was gone for days before coming home tonight, and made your sad mother wait.

You're too young to know what luxury is. Let me tell you. Luxury is washing your feet so your civilized wife will think you're a decent man. Luxury is drinking cold water and breathing in fresh air. And look. There's your mother now, hurrying to turn off the lights so my luxury can be hers tonight.

April 2
Jung-in, your daddy met a great man last night. He's a writer. But that's not what makes him great. He's a man who knows how to love. He's given me so much. You don't have any belongings to call your own yet, so you don't know how hard it is to share what you have. Whenever I meet a great man like this writer, I don't want to leave his side. I'm so happy I get to live in the same world as he. Although I'm not a great man myself.

I know so little, and I'm not a smart man. But I will be content knowing you'll read this one day and laugh at your poor father's foolishness. Your mother removed a mole from my face. If a mole pops up near your eye, I'll remove it for you. But if it reappears on my face, Jung-in, it won't ever go away.

April 13
I have so much I want to say, but my mind's going dark on me, Jung-in. I wanted to write about poetry tonight, Jung-in, about love, about misspelled poems, about misspelled lives. Maybe you can ask your mother later.

That was the last of the entries. There were a few more scribbles, but the letters were too smudged or blotched to read.

I still remember the date, April 13, he came home drunk for the second night in a row. He couldn't wake up the next morning. I took the last apple from the fridge and along with a carrot, grated it and made freshly squeezed juice, just like I used to make for our daughter. When I helped him up, his eyes stayed closed, as if he were too tired to lift his eyelids. He drank the juice and went back to sleep. When he woke up, he announced a craving for *kimchi* fried rice seasoned with sesame oil and wrapped in seaweed. I made it for him.

He often made these bizarre requests. "I want to eat the kind of meal you crave when it's summer, and you've taken a nap after your mother yelled at you for something, and you wake up and you're heading over to the kitchen for dinner when your family calls you into the living room instead, and, as you're turning to go, suddenly a drop of water falls on your forehead. What would I crave at a moment like that?"

After finishing the seaweed rice, he checked his watch and saw it was past two o'clock. I was wiping the table. Suddenly, he drew me close, and whispered, "Poor woman." He looked down at our sleeping daughter and brought his nose to her. Several strands of her hair fluttered in the air from his nostrils. He sat there for a long time.

Finally getting to his feet, he started getting ready for work. I gave him a wad of cash, which I don't normally do. He stared down at it, before letting out a long sigh. I thought he needed something more, so I walked him to the bus stop, with Jung-in in my arms. He let the first bus go. When the second bus came, he sighed, "I guess I should go, huh?" After staring down at his feet for the longest time, he forced himself to climb into the bus. As the bus was about to leave, he looked back, and whispered, "I really don't want to go." His eyes looked dark and sad as he peered out the window at his waving daughter.

I stood there for a while after the bus left. I stared down at my old shoes the same way he did a few minutes ago, before wrapping the blanket firmly around Jung-in and getting on a bus for a beauty salon three stops away. I haven't changed my hair in a year, and knew it wouldn't affect how he felt. But I knew of no other way to help him carry his weight.

That night, he didn't come home.

On the day before he left on his trip, he announced his arrival home by kicking the door. When I opened it, he fell face forward. Thinking back to that now, I realize he'd already made up his mind to go on the trip. He was about to say goodbye to everything he loved.

After laying him on the sofa, I was about to turn in myself when some force tugged me back. When I turned around, the hair on the back of my neck stood up. My husband was sitting straight up on the sofa. He looked unreal, almost, like a frozen corpse or a spirit detached from its body. What gave me chills was the faint glimmer of light near his knee. He was holding a small lighter in his hands. It shone between his fingers. It was fire.

He laughed, his teeth flashing white in the gleam of the fire. It floated upward before landing on some paper on the glass-topped table, which burst into flame. He threw the lighter across the room, cackling maniacally.

I heard a low gasp from behind me. Our daughter had awakened. She was staring at the fire in his hand.

"Mommy, fire came out of daddy," she spoke in a hushed voice.

The next morning, I gathered the ashes and torn bits of newspaper, wiping out the previous night's memory. He hasn't come home since then.

It's been two weeks since he left on this trip.

I'd like to explain why I'm so upset that he's gone. His journey is not of this world. He left his body here, taking only his soul. His discarded body lies in front of me, on the corner bed of this four-patient hospital room. His two eyes remain stubbornly closed beneath the tightly bound bandages. He's not planning on coming back anytime soon. Or perhaps he's waiting until the bruises from last night's car crash subside into a dull yellow.

But he will come back. He'll run out in the middle of the night looking for new notebooks and pens again. He'll come back to writing letters to his young daughter before giving that up, too. He will come back. He always said that growing old with me was his holy hope.

I started knitting last week. Day and night, I sat by his bed knitting him a sweater. I know I'll be the first person he asks for when he wakes up, which is why I can't leave his side He likes it when I knit for him. If he saw me knitting, I thought, he wouldn't dare go back to where he was.

I'd measured the sweater against his body so many times that it felt like I'd seen him wearing it. The sweater felt like part of his body.

The day I began knitting the sleeves, I looked down at the sweater and let out a silent scream. The body and two sleeves of the sweater looked like dismembered limbs and a torso sprawled out on the sheets. I knitted furiously to finish it so it'd be whole and intact.

When I finished it, however, I thought he might not like it. He doesn't like clothes with a slim fit. I unraveled it and started over.

Finally, the sweater is finished. Trying to ignore the soreness in my back and shoulders, and rubbing the calluses on my fingers, I speak to him. I can hear him saying how much he hates the sweater. 'The neck is too narrow. It's too tight around the neck.' I pull out the yarn and knit it over again. 'What about now?' He scoffs. 'You'll never get it. Don't try to force me into your sweater. I'm not changing myself for you.'

It almost feels as if he's here with me; he just hasn't entered his body yet.

Once when I was little, I got in trouble for drawing a mustache on my brother's face when he was sleeping. My mother said I'd changed his face so much that his soul might not recognize him after leaving his body during a nap. My husband might be back already; his soul just hasn't found his body yet. I remove his hospital clothes. My hands are shaking.

His skin feels warm. He used to come home with fresh bruises before his old bruises could properly heal, but there are no new bruises on him now. His body is clean. No bruises! Frantically, I search his chest, his stomach, his arms and legs. His body is so white, so translucent.

I stop searching.

There are no traces of bruising.

4

Was fate still toying with Chung and Hyun? A few days later, they both called me.

Chung called first.

"Young's dead." His voice sounded shocked more than sad. "The idiot was full of surprises until the very end. He died. Just like that. Over a month ago." I could almost picture Chung shaking his head.

I was quiet for a while. "Did they have a funeral?"

"It was kept small and private. They scattered his ashes over a lake," he sighed. "We talked about him the last time we met. Little did we know we were talking about a dead man."

I was silent.

"He should have stayed alive," Chung continued. "At least then he might have had another opportunity to prove himself. Miserable fuck."

His words trailed off. He told me some of the alums were pooling cash for Young's family, as Young, ever the "free spirit," had left no money behind. Chung didn't mention that this idea was his.

Holding a fundraiser for him after his death will only make his incompetence official, I think, but don't say out loud.

The dead aren't extended the courtesy to refuse unwanted charity. They can't put up fights when their lives are redefined and reinterpreted by the living. Of course, the dead don't care about redeeming themselves. Mourning the dead is only a way for the living to make themselves feel better.

Hyun called that evening. At first, I thought it was a wrong number. She hesitated for a long time, and her voice didn't sound clear on the phone.

"Who's this? Who's calling?" I asked sleepily, as my eyes skimmed the newspaper. When she mentioned "Traces of Bruising," I put down the paper and turned to face the window. It was already dark outside.

Out of nowhere, images appeared across the window, as if someone had flipped a switch for the floodlights illuminating a stage. I saw Hyun as she was in college, setting her aluminum tray on a cafeteria table and smoothing back her hair. Her cheeks are snowy white. Soft downy hair forms a fringe along her ears, which are adorned with tiny gold drop earrings. She's wearing a crimson dress with a round collar and white belt. I see Young splitting a pair of wooden chopsticks. With an exaggerated motion, he trims the rough edges before handing them to Hyun with a wide grin.

Back in my office, Hyun is speaking nervously over the phone, "You're married, of course? Do you have children? My husband told me so much about you." She spoke as if we'd never met before. It took me a while to catch what she was getting at, that she wanted her manuscript back. "I'm actually calling from a pay phone outside your campus."

"Why don't you come to my office?" I asked. "It's in the west wing, room 304. I can wait downstairs for you."

"Actually, I was hoping maybe we could meet at a café somewhere instead…"

"But we're near a college campus. The cafés are all crowded and noisy."

"Yes, but still, I'd prefer that, if you don't mind…" She was polite, but firm.

After hanging up, I looked down at my newspaper again. One article read, *87% of Erectile Dysfunction Stems from Psychological Causes.* Next to it was

Why Does Autumn Bring the Blues? The article argued that we get depressed in the fall because our bodies haven't adjusted to the temperature change. My wife was probably at the doctor's office right now. Unconsciously, I brought a hand to my lips, something I hadn't done since quitting smoking that spring. Health-conscious articles such as this played a role in my decision to quit smoking. Turning off the computer, I slowly got up from my chair.

When I stepped into the warm air inside the café, my glasses fogged up. Taking them off, I scanned the room and saw a woman awkwardly getting up from her seat near the entrance. When I took a step toward her, she sat back down, relieved I'd seen her.

I put my glasses back on and gaped in surprise. I removed them again and taking my seat, began wiping them with a small piece of cloth. She waited patiently for me to finish. She was wearing a crimson dress with a white collar and a white patent leather belt. When the server came, she smoothed back her hair with one hand. Her earlobe sparkled gold. She looked like time had plucked her from our campus twenty years ago and placed her before me.

"You've changed so little I almost didn't recognize you," I finally managed.

"You mean this dress? Oh... Well, it still fits, so I kept it." She smiled. Only then did I see the faintest suggestion of wrinkles around her eyes and mouth. When she brought the cup to her lips, I noticed how the sleeves of her dress have faded near the cuff from years of washing. But when she looked up at me, the whites of her eyes were so clean and pure they were tinged blue.

"I'm sorry for inconveniencing you like this," she began apologetically.

"You're taking back the manuscript?"

"Yes." She lowered her head and played with her mug. I felt the college girls sitting at the bar glancing at me. I briefly considered what I should do in the event Hyun started crying, but her face remained impassive.

"It all seemed so futile," she finally spoke.

"I'm sorry?"

"When our old friends offered their help."

I remained quiet.

"I didn't need any help," she continued. "No one understood my husband." She ran her tongue across her lips a few times, but didn't cry.

"Everyone thinks he was weak, but he held himself together when he could have completely let himself go. Doesn't that mean he's strong? I could never do what he did. If I were as strong or honest as he was, I'd have left him a long time ago."

She took the manuscript from the manila folder I'd brought. Her hands were rough and gnarled, a stark contrast to her waiflike frame. I couldn't make out her expression, but I understood what her hands were trying to say. I watched as they smoothed the cover page of the manuscript before coming to rest over the word "bruising." Suddenly, she flinched. I had accidentally left my letter opener inside the folder. It slipped out and onto her hand. She pressed the letter opener to her palm, as if trying to warm it.

"Do you agree with the others?" she asked.

"What do you mean?"

"He tried... hard. He did the best he could." Getting up from her seat, she tucked the letter opener into the folder. Deliberately.

After paying for the tea, I went outside to find her staring down at her shoes. She looked up and asked, "Does that letter opener belong to you?"

"Huh? Yes, yes, it's mine."

"He had the same one. Did you buy it at the Inca exhibit?"

However different I thought I was from Young, our lives had intersected in that way, at least.

I came home to find my wife lying in bed.

"I went to the doctor today," she said.

"Are you okay?"

"Yes."

"Good."

She looked haggard. When I pulled the sheets up to her chin, she smiled wanly and said, "We need to talk."

I sat down at the edge of the bed.

"Did you think I was afraid?" she asked.

"I thought you were angry at me. Weren't you?"

"No. I was just afraid. I..."

I waited quietly for her to continue.

"I was confused. I didn't know whether I wanted a baby or not. There must be more me's inside of me than the woman I know. Sometimes, I don't even know who I am."

She spoke for a long time.

"Even I couldn't know all of me, so I made a decision. I decided to live as the 'me' I know best. When I reached that conclusion, I immediately felt peace. Everything felt much easier. The doctor told me it's better to forget the decision once it's been made, and I think he was right."

From her words, I couldn't tell whether it was a psychiatrist or an ob-gyn she had seen that day. I inched closer to her to ask. She forced a smile and reached out for my hand. There was a small bruise on the back of her hand where the needle had pierced her skin.

Nobody Checks the Time When They're Happy

I Loved Your Laughter

The first thing I do every morning is throw open the curtains to let the light into my basement apartment. If you saw me shivering, leaning against the window, barefoot, in my thin pajamas, you'd probably think I was cold. And if you saw me make toast at an ungodly hour, very slowly spread peanut butter on the toast, then throw the knife on the table and bolt upright in my seat, you'd think I was lonely. But you're wrong. Because do you know what I do afterward? I run to my room, open the second drawer of my mom's old vanity, and dig for Q-tips. Imagine me, swallowing hard and working a Q-tip in one ear, blinking at how it tickles. And as I do this, I hear your laughter inside of me.

We went to the movies once, like other couples do. You wore your glasses. As soon as we found our seats, you took out your glasses case, which I promptly plucked from your hands. Carefully, I removed your glasses, as if I were reaching inside your chest for your heart. It was a joy to wipe those glasses of yours, and it thrilled me that you were silently studying my every move, the light from the screen illuminating your changing facial expressions.

You know what else I liked? Your brown shoes, with the tiny eight holes on either side of the laces. They were so smooth. I remember how they kept coming untied—the shoelaces, that is. You exclaimed, *Look, my shoelaces are dragging again*, like a happy little boy who'd stumbled upon a silver coin on the ground. I liked bending down to tie your shoelaces for you, your foot propped up on a nearby flowerpot. Would I still have liked it if you hadn't playfully breathed down my neck each time?

You knew I liked the white half-moons of your nails, the scar on your left knee, the tiny wrinkles that formed on your nose when you smiled, the way you walked with hunched shoulders as if battling perpetual cold weather, your long, full gait. You knew how much I liked them. And yet you had to go and die on me. You bastard.

I didn't go to my job at the hair salon today. Is it Sunday? If so, why haven't I turned on the TV? Why am I in bed staring at the wallpaper's pattern? I took the day off because I have the flu. My boss is no doubt annoyed about canceling my appointments, but these days, I don't feel like working. I keep dropping the scissors, and the blow-dryer feels so heavy in my hand. Did I tell you? When I was little, my shoulder was dislocated twice. Perhaps that had something to do with it when, not long ago, I was about to comb neutralizer into a customer's hair when I accidentally poured it over her face. Once, I dropped a plastic bowl full of ammonium on the floor. Fortunately, the mixture was so thick it didn't spill. It's the same white solution we use to straighten hair. Remember? The one you said reminded you of shaving cream? You smeared some on my nose and cheeks once. You said every time you had buttered rolls, you were reminded of the syrupy liquid. Speaking of food, it's already past noon and I haven't had breakfast yet. There's probably some bread in the fridge.

When I called my boss to tell her I was staying home, she was reassuring. "Get some rest. And if you don't feel any better, go see a doctor. Are you coming in tomorrow?"

Everyone's concerned about me. They were concerned two years ago when my mom died, too. My boss must think my grief is what's preventing me from leaving the house. She'll still mark today as unpaid leave, though. She didn't like it when you came to the salon to wait for me, flipping through magazines with the rest of our customers. Now that you're dead, she feels guilty. Why are people so generous toward the dead? Everyone thinks death is bad news, and they cry about how unfortunate it is, but is the dead person missing out on anything? Is the world that fantastic?

True, the dead don't get any tomorrows. People discuss tomorrow in hopeful tones, as in, tomorrow brings new opportunities, tomorrow's a brand new day, the sun will come up tomorrow, etc. But does tomorrow really bring hope? To me, tomorrow means suffering through mind-numbing pop music and inhaling bleach fumes while wrestling with damaged hair and sweating from the heat of blow-dryers. Tomorrow means wolfing down a quick lunch of tofu soup or noodles in the employees' room and massaging the deluded egos of customers. There's also the bitchy boss to deal with, who grew increasingly embittered as the economy soured. But all that's fine. You can't expect to make money without jumping through at least some hoops. But do you know why my hope's gone? It's because tomorrow will come, and you won't be there. That's taken away my hope. It would be nice if we could travel back in time so that after today, instead of tomorrow, we had yesterday. Then you'd still be alive. My past hasn't been a bed of roses, so at least I know what happens. Nothing will surprise me. I won't be afraid.

Basically, your death cost me more than it cost you.

The bread's cold and hard. I should stick it in the toaster. I press the switch, and immediately, the coils glow red. Click! Out pops the toast, peeking out of the white toaster oven. I'd set the timer for thirty seconds, so that's exactly how much time has passed. Are you checking your watch by any chance? You had the bad habit of doubting the surest of events. Your watch broke often, and your explanation was that our bodies cast a unique magnetic field that refuses to align with the world's time zones. Let's be honest. Your watches broke because they were cheap. I've seen at least a dozen die on you.

I can feel your eyes staring at me. Is it because I said the word *die*? You don't like me tossing that word around so casually. I'm sorry. I'll try not to. My mom said I used that word as a kid when a home appliance broke. The lamp died, I'd say. Or the phone's dead. The radio's dead. Curiously, I never used it to describe appliances that were just resting, like a toaster oven slipping back into inactivity once the toast was done. I must have sensed that some things know when to go silent. Silence isn't symptomatic of death. No, death arrives unexpectedly. If we could set our lives on timers, when would you want your life to end? In thirty years? Forty? I guess this question is meaningless to you, since you died at twenty-four—before you could even play this hypothetical game. You must see missing out on the game as a loss. After all, you chose to spend your life doing random, useless things. You probably never imagined for a second you'd die so young.

You were found dead inside a phone booth way out in a park by the river. You had no IDs on you, just some cash in your pockets. Fortunately, the police found my eyeglasses case and called the number of the shop stamped inside. They found me working in the salon upstairs from the eyewear shop. I offered the detectives green tea. I was trying to process what I'd heard. Could it be true that you killed yourself? Why would you do that?

That's what the police wanted to know, too, but I didn't know what to tell them. I got so sick of their questions that I wanted to blurt out that your watches always died. I wanted to ask if your watch was still running when they found you. The police complained you'd made more work for them because you didn't leave behind a note. They also mentioned they found a photograph in your other pocket, but they didn't show it to me.

In any case, there was nothing I could do. It would be a thousand times better if you were alive, but you're not, so all I can do is love a dead person. I can't stop loving you just because you're dead. The love's there. Where would it go? Did I tell you I used to gaze for hours at tea kettles whistling on the stove? I was fascinated and saddened by the white steam disappearing into thin air. Where does it go? Later in science class, when I learned that steam doesn't actually disappear but in fact converts to another state and remains permanently part of this world, I was ecstatic. Death is just another state. Yes, it'll be a little challenging to love you now that you're not physically here, but that doesn't scare me. What scares me is the thought I might forget you. Because if I do, it'll mean I've lost my love. And we all know everyone only gets one love per lifetime.

The toast smells good. It'd be nice if you were here.

Death was Always a Shadow

I'm going through my photo albums again. There are pictures of my mom, and of my father, too. They're together in some of the pictures. Am I in them? No. Because my father died before I was born. No amount of effort can place me in pictures with a father who died four months before I was born.

I'm sure you remember the first night we spent together in this room. That's when you saw the albums.

It was raining that night. The humidity lent a coldness to your body that I shivered to touch. A shock of your slick, wet hair spilled over your forehead. I don't know how many minutes passed as we sat there, wordlessly listening to the gray drumming of the rain. Suddenly, you asked me why I never wore bras. That's when I told you about my mom. "Last spring, when we were cremating her..."

I told you how we finally got around to burning all her possessions and the fumes stung my eyes so bad I started to cry. She had more clothes than anything else. Outdated ones, long past their prime. A white linen blouse with grapes appliqued near the breast. A pleated pink skirt with half the pleats undone. Mom used to wear them before she was married. Her costume jewelry, purses, and hats were all faded and worn. Mom could never throw anything away; she took her hoarded junk with her each time we moved, which was often. I guess you could say she was fashionable. I'm more of a flannel-and-jeans kind of girl. Hair always in a bob. But Mom was different. She grew out her hair and arranged it every night in faded curlers she stored in an old plastic basket. That is, until she was hospitalized.

Mom tried to teach me to dress more like a lady. You can guess how I took to that, seeing as how I couldn't even stand her ladylike ways. I still shudder to think of the things she bought me in high school. You wanted to know why I never wear bras. I'm getting to that. I hated how uncomfortable they were, but more than that, the skin where the elastic band rubbed against used to swell a bright angry red, leaving me scratching at the welts all night until they bled. I had to wear bras though, since our home economics teacher inspected us daily for improper attire, but mom took it further and insisted I wear girdles and what looked like yards of rubber taped around my body. *Pain is beauty,* she cooed, stressing the importance of molding my body into a "pretty" figure before the bones could set. I yelled back, saying I'd rather hand-write the Bible with my own blood and feed it to mosquitoes than force myself into a socially-acceptable body. I snarled that having one woman in the family endure the pains of womanhood was enough. Mom burst out crying.

We fought often over the TV remote, too. I liked soap operas, but mom preferred fancy theatrical shows with fog made with dry ice spilling off the stage. That's not all. Whenever I took her to dinner on pay day, she squealed for a "Western" restaurant. Once there, she sighed over the expensive courses scrawled in fancy writing on the menu's front pages and studied the listings thoroughly. Not once did she order a full course.

She was a horrible cook. Even after all those years, her rice came out invariably too wet or too dry and the *kimchi* either too sour or too raw, the garlic and ginger never properly infusing with the peppers. Her excuse was that *kimchi* has always been notoriously difficult to make and that's why women traditionally made it in groups. Imagine how she fared as a housekeeper. She was once hired by a doctor's family as a housekeeper and nanny to the couple's five-year-old daughter. She was fired almost immediately. Apparently, she spent all her time shopping with the little girl for pretty bows and frilly socks instead of doing the housework. The owners, who were initially taken by her sophisticated manners, later shook their heads and showed her the door. There was literally nothing she was good at, except crying. She was the queen of tears. I could live with the fact that we were poor; what I couldn't stand was mom crying over how poor we were. Maybe the reason I don't cry is because I grew so sick of her tears. Or maybe I used up all my tears crying with her during her fits so there are no tears left to shed.

But don't assume I didn't love her. Before I met you, she was the only person I ever loved. You two should have met. You would have fallen more in love with me for having a mom who was still gorgeous at fifty.

When I finished telling you about my mom, you sat up in bed and brought your lips to mine. Then you asked if I had any pictures of her. You said you wanted to see them. Your eyes were smiling, your voice was warm with love. Pulling the sheets up to my chest, I got up to retrieve the photo albums. With each step I took toward the desk, the sheets pulled away from your body. We began a mock tug-of-war—you fighting to keep enough of the sheets to cover your crotch as I fought to shield my nakedness. Remember that? The sheets became so taut it looked like we were pitching a tent.

It was still raining, and night was wearing on. Rain fell thickly and darkness pressed in on our window, cocooning us in our own little world. Both of us completely naked, we snuggled under the sheets with the photo albums, like impoverished siblings waiting for their parents to come home from work. Siblings? If we were that, I guess I'd be your older sister since I'm a year older.

Why are there so many albums? you asked, and I pointed out that I had two more boxes of photographs I hadn't found the time to organize.

"I photograph well. Photographers say the camera loves me," I said.

Emitting a low whistle, you chuckled, "That makes two of us."

"You and the photographer?"

"Me and the camera."

68

Why did we fight that night? You went quiet as soon as we flipped to the album's first page. The strangest expression came over your face when I pointed out one of the pre-marriage pictures of my mom and her friends. You looked more incredulous than anything. It was obvious you were upset. You were silent until the last page. It didn't seem like you were looking at the photographs anymore. And the thunder was so loud. I asked what was wrong, but you didn't respond. You fell back on the bed as soon as I turned the last page. I asked you again. "Don't you like looking at photographs?"

"Photographs can be a terrible thing." Your voice sounded heavy. Nervous, and also a little hurt, I argued back, "Photographs are a record of time. Without them, people like me with horrible memories who never keep journals won't have a way to remember the past."

Slowly, you asked, "Remember the past? For what?"

"For..." My voice trailed off. I used to be seized by anger when you asked questions that seemed insanely obvious.

You murmured, "Why do people want to capture the past? It's not like the past can serve as an alibi."

Outraged, I briefly considered breaking up with you, but I knew I could never do it. I'd already fallen in love with your ears and how shiny they always were—as if you'd just stepped out of the shower. How could I leave you when just minutes ago, you were wrapped in my arms? I didn't break up with you. Instead, I got my revenge by staying stubbornly attached to photography. Was it last January when we went to Jang-hung on a rainy day? You acquiesced to my constant plea for pictures. Your heart's at least ten times softer than what you give it credit for; I knew that from the beginning. You took pictures of me in a café by the dock even as the owner scowled at us. As far as revenge goes though, this wasn't a complete one, because you didn't let me take any pictures of you.

The thought is depressing me again. I should have made you pose for at least one, or maybe even snuck in a furtive shot. Maybe I should look through my photos to see if you were captured anywhere in the background. But I realize it's useless. After all, you were always the one behind the camera, and during our entire time together, you never took your eyes off me. Just like the camera.

You're looking at me now, aren't you?

Come closer. I want us to go back to that night and look through the albums again. You know what's strange? For all that mocking about photographs, you had a picture with you in your pocket when you died. Why? Whatever. Never mind. You can't upset me anymore. You're dead. You can't assert yourself anymore. You're dead. You can't change. You can't leave me. You're now utterly, entirely mine. Mine to keep suspended in time in my own little freezer. So stop complaining and come look at this first photograph with me. It was taken before my mom and dad fell in love.

Photo 1: The Blissful Days of Mom's Youth

This must have been taken at the shore.

Three girls are standing in the front row, with two, four, no, five guys standing behind them. The girls' long hair is fluttering in the breeze. All three are dressed in crisp flared skirts and white blouses. It couldn't have been easy to pose with sand up to the heels of their sandals, but their smiles are as fresh and joyful as the sun.

The girl on the right, her body lurching slightly forward, is a little heavier than the others. She's also the only one without sunglasses, and she's posing with one hand daringly placed on her hip. Obviously, this one's got personality. Compared to her, the other two look decidedly prim. The girl on the left has strong features, with deep sunken eyes and a narrow, sharp nose. Her face betrays a scheming, jealous nature. Despite her smile, she's nervously fingering the beads of her necklace. What's that? You think I can read faces? I suppose you can say I do. After all, my job as a hairstylist involves having to decipher women's expressions all day long.

The girl in the middle looks so sweet and lovely. She's dressed like the others, but the polka dot hairband and matching belt give her outfit a pop of color. Do you see her plump, porcelain arms and toothy smile? And look at her bare feet in those sandals.

See the man standing between the chubby girl and the girl in the middle? The tall guy in neatly ironed slacks, the one grinning next to the middle girl's sunshade? Don't you admire his high forehead, his playful grin? That's my father. He's the only one that catches your eyes. The guy to his left in the colorful shirt is completely unremarkable. And the man on the far left, standing about a foot away from the others? You can't call him unremarkable. With his thick eyebrows and that faraway look in his eyes, I suppose you could say he has an aura of sultriness. He's the only one who's not smiling, and because his face is slightly in profile, the shadows playing on his face lend him a brooding, sensitive look. But notice the lock of hair falling over his forehead and the long fingers curved around his thigh? He's one of those insufferable passive aggressive types. I bet he's either from a poor family or chock full of insecurities. What's that? You think he's got a story to tell? Whatever. I don't like him. He looks indecisive.

The three girls and five guys all look to be in their early twenties, don't they? They're bursting with eager anticipation, like the bouncing beach balls they sell at beachfront stores. Sunlight gleams in streaks above the women's sunshades, as if a child threw fistfuls of sand into the air, letting the grains scatter and pause for just a second in the light. They're framed by a background of pine trees, sky, and clouds.

You've probably guessed, correctly, that the girl in the middle is my mom. Can you also see that all five guys were obviously in love with her? The other girls, the trees, and the sky are, in fact, flanking her, putting her at center stage. The men are either looking at her or hoping to catch her eye. My dad's arm can't be seen in the picture; maybe he's got it slyly positioned around her waist. And the brooding man? He's in love with her, too, though he's trying to hide it. The other two girls are there to make her look all the more desirable. Do you blame the sky, clouds and wind for wanting to be near her? Everything is bearing witness to her incredible beauty.

It's afternoon, and the sand is hot. After posing for the photograph, the girls must have dropped their sunshades, laughing loudly in the sun. The men probably ran ahead to the pine forest to spread blankets on the ground for the girls. They might have burst out in song. Mom couldn't carry a tune to save her life, but she loves to clap and nod along. I'm sure everyone gazed at her with love. The sun began to set. They felt the wind through blouses damp with sweat. Time passed the way it does during rounds of "duck, duck, goose."

Have you ever played that game—"duck, duck, goose"? Where the one who's "it" stealthily drops a towel behind his victim, who remains oblivious to what's going on until it's too late? Everyone else sees where the towel is. Realizing the victim is completely clueless, the others sing and clap in a frenzy. Only then does the victim turn around and discover the unlucky towel.

That's what happened to my mom. She was too busy cheering and clapping to notice fate creeping up on her. Even as the towel was twisting itself around her, she was muttering to herself, "No, this can't be. This can't be the story of my life. This has to be a dream. When I wake up from this nightmare, my real life will begin. And it's going to be a great life." When she finally sensed her fate, it was too late.

Oh, I almost forgot. You remember the chubby girl next to my mom? She's your aunt.

When she came to visit my mom at the hospital, I was so exhausted I thought I was hallucinating: a hippopotamus in a dress. She burst out sobbing the minute she saw my mom. She wheezed louder than the hospital air conditioner. My mom, who's usually the one doing the sobbing, adjusted the knitted cap on her head before opening with a dignified, "It's been a while since I last saw you. How did you know I was here?" Chemotherapy had left her bald and emaciated, so her attempts at dignity seemed almost sad, like watching a plucked peacock trying to show off its feathers.

"Is this your daughter? I barely recognize her," your aunt croaked through her tears. Turning to me, she asked, "Do you remember me? Maybe you don't. I last saw you many years ago, almost twenty years!"

Turning back to my mom, she smiled, "Your daughter refused to have her picture taken that day, remember? You had to drag her into the picture and ended up dislocating her shoulder. She was a stubborn little thing! But look how well she's grown up."

With a dreamy look in her eyes, mom replied, "Oh, you mean the day we took your nephew to Changkyung Palace. He must have grown up, too."

"Yes, he looks just like his father. He drove me here, actually. He's waiting outside. I can invite him in, if you'd like."

"Don't bother. It'll only make him uncomfortable," my mom shook her head sadly.

I saw you for the first time when I walked your aunt out to the hallway to see her off. You were smoking, your back turned to me, with two motorcycle helmets perched on a windowsill. Picturing your fat aunt sitting behind you on your motorcycle with her head squished into one of those helmets, I couldn't help but stifle a laugh.

"Here, let me introduce you," your aunt offered. At the sound of her voice, you slowly turned toward me. The afternoon sun created a veil of dust motes and light between us, momentarily blinding me. I had to take a step back. Almost at the same time, you took a step back as well. We stood like that for a moment, no longer than a few seconds. But to me, it felt much longer. Time must have a density to it, too, the way hair straightening solution refuses to pour when it's been mixed too thick.

"You met once before, but you probably don't remember since you were so little at the time." Your aunt's voice came from far away. "You even pinky swore to marry one another when you grew up. Did you forget?"

I felt dizzy as I walked you and your aunt to the hospital entrance. I've always been slightly anemic. My legs tottered weakly as I followed you down the stairs. You were silent, too. Only your aunt went on and on about the past. She and my mom, as well as your mom, were part of a group of seven girls who'd been close throughout high school. I nodded. I remembered seeing a photograph in my mom's album with seven girls in uniforms standing shoulder to shoulder with "The Forbidden Seven" captioned below in cursive.

Your aunt was just as eager to brag about your accomplishments. She told me how your mother wanted you to take the civil service exam to work in government like your father did until he was killed in that tragic plane accident, but that you preferred music and wanted to study conducting in graduate school. I nodded. The gifted son with a rebellious streak. I was familiar with the type. I'd seen it in soap operas. What seemed unreal, however, was when your aunt suddenly announced, "I need to use the ladies' room before we leave." That's when you turned to me and asked, "May I call you?"

I snorted, "What for?" Secretly, I felt ready to faint from joy and nerves, which happens often in soap operas, too.

Photograph 2: Mom as New Bride, Attends His Engagement Party

In this second picture, the date is written in white italics. February 14, 1974.

That was an eventful year. My parents got married in January, and my dad died in August. I was born in December. This picture was taken less than a month after my mom and dad's marriage. They were at a friend's engagement party. Look at the people in this picture. They're the friends from the shore photograph, minus two people.

The couple in the middle are the bride and groom. The woman is the temperamental girl from the first picture with the striking features. As for the man, I bet you didn't recognize him in those glasses. He's that solemn guy from the beach, the one with the faraway look in his eyes. Do you see how happy the bride-to-be looks? She almost looks smug. She's leaning so far toward her fiancé that my mom, sitting to her right, looks snubbed. One of her white-gloved hands is on my mom's wrist, not as a show of friendship but as a caution. Half of her hair has been styled into a teased bun, with the rest blow-dried and falling past her shoulders. I'm familiar with the type of women who like that look. They're vain and fake. She has so much stray hair that her stylist probably had to tack dozens of pins into the bun. Women with a lot of stray hair are usually difficult to get along with. You think I'm being too hard on her? What do you care? You don't know her.

Her fiancé, on the other hand, is a little too composed, a little sad, even. He still has that faraway look in his eye. I don't know if it's the glint in his glasses but it looks almost as if he's looking at my mom, not his fiancée.

My mom, now a wife, is dressed in *hanbok* with her hair in an up-do, giving her a more mature look. Her laughter, formerly so bursting with life, has been replaced with a thin smile. In the shore picture, she was glowing from the sun and the wind. This picture has drooping willow branches in the background. There's also a small bridge leading up to a distant pagoda, which speaks of nostalgia and star-crossed paths. My mom's eyes are tinged with a knowing sadness. Do you see the thin gold necklace around her neck? She never took that off, except for the two times she had surgery.

When I got the news that my mom had cancer, I assumed she'd soon be cured. Not long after, I learned she only had a few months left. How could that be? I've read stories of people who were struck by a fatal disease just when their lives were starting to look up, like the unlucky widow who suddenly collapsed and died after her children left the nest, leaving her free for the first time in her life. I wondered whether I'd stolen my mom's share of luck by being the only one in my beauty school class to get a job, as if there's a limit to the amount of luck one family is allotted and I've maxed out ours. It's like where two children take the same test but only one kid passes, and where two sisters go into labor and only one of them has a son. I thought that was just an old wives' tale. And it wasn't as if Mom was a chaste widow. I didn't mention this before, but she didn't love my father. She loved the brooding man in the glasses.

On the day my father proposed to her, she went to see that man in his shabby apartment. Telling him what happened, she confessed that her love was for him, not my father. But the man told her he couldn't promise her anything. Devastated, she married my dad.

Imagine how it must have felt attending the engagement party of the man she loved. One side of her wanted to see the look on his face when she showed up as the happy young wife, and the other side yearned to see the man she adored. Added to that were feelings of intense guilt and jealousy.

The party continued at the bride-to-be's house. Mom kept drinking despite the fact she couldn't hold down a drink. She laughed hard and cried harder. Often, she dabbed at her eyes with the silk scarf hanging from her neck. Sometimes, the scarf would still be at her eye when she'd hear a funny story and burst out laughing. Her laughter shone as brightly as it did in the shore photo, when neither she nor the man she loved was married, when nothing had been decided and everything was possible. How could she have known that her fate was about to unleash itself upon her? Even in this second photograph, she had no clue about what was lurking behind her.

When they found themselves alone outside, the man hugged her shoulders from behind. Mom looked down at the shadow of the huge persimmon tree in front of her. She saw his shadow bearing down on her. Every time the wind rustled, the persimmon leaves whispered angry curses at them. Mom's flushed cheeks slowly cooled. When he reached out and grabbed her necklace, she grew weak in his arms. That necklace was a gift from him. Nothing excuses her decision to appear at his engagement party married to another man yet wearing the necklace he gave her. When he brought his burning lips to hers, she succumbed. That night, she became pregnant with me.

That's why Mom never tried to hide her tears. I'm the stain left by the man who ruined her life that night, not the semen spilled on her petticoat. Imagine how terrified she must have been upon learning she was pregnant. But as luck would have it, around the time she began to show, my father died in an accident. Mom was so stunned by fate's speedy maneuvers that sorrow slipped away from her. All she could think of was whether to conceal the truth and live as a single mother or to unravel fate's twisted ball and reveal the truth to the baby's father.

Many friends attended my father's funeral. The funeral of a twenty-eight-year-old is an event too traumatic and pathetic to miss. The brooding man was there, too, with his fiancée by his side. Since they'd come as guests, Mom kept her head respectfully bowed without meeting their eyes. He saw her necklace. His fiancée saw mom's soft, pale neck. She followed Mom into the kitchen and, removing a wedding invitation from her beaded purse, thrust it into my mom's shaking hands. The wedding was set for the coming month.

Mom didn't look at him once. He didn't join the men playing cards. He sat by himself, staring blankly at the letters on the banners spelling "Funeral—Kang Hyung" and "Leaving the Concerns of This World." Like you, he was a heavy smoker. Mom says he always had a cigarette between his fingers.

Mom cried so much at the burial that she brought out sobs from the other guests. She crumpled to the floor when they carried the coffin out of the house. It was part theatrics, like showing up at her lover's engagement party to show off how happy she was. Except this time, grief, not joy, was her weapon of choice. Sadly, her intentions were misread, as everyone at the burial—including him—assumed the cries were for her late husband. He left the funeral quietly mocking himself for planning to tell her how he felt.

Wasn't my mom a terrible fool for losing her chance? And wasn't he? But really, there was nothing they could possibly do to fight a fate that had already been written.

You don't believe in fate, do you? You said so yourself. You said if anything horrible happened, you'd thumb your nose at fate. I used to feel the same way. I thought fate was an excuse concocted by unhappy people, but now, I'm not so sure. Why does my life have to run parallel with death's shadow? How can I explain this coincidence without turning to fate? Why did you have to die? Did you get sick of setting your watch? Did you want to leave me? No, that can't be it. Fate has to be the only explanation. I must infect the people I love with the parasite of death. Fate has cursed me.

Time and Happiness

I just made coffee.

I take mine sweet and go through about half a dozen cups a day. According to one women's magazine, the three-cup-a-day mark is the line drawn between a treat and an addiction. Be that as it may, this habit is the only thing that keeps me going at work. My mom used to scold me for drinking coffee even on my days off, when she gorged on aspirin and Pepto Bismol. She hated to think. Often, she waved away my questions, feigning forgetfulness, or insisted the drugs were making her brain foggy. Though her short-term memory was scant, she nevertheless kept a strong hold on memories.

How much of your childhood do you remember? From what age? My mom swore her recollections became more vivid as she grew older. After she turned fifty, she claimed to remember her grandfather smiling and beckoning to her when she was two years old. For my part, I remember her constantly leafing through the photo albums in all the apartments we lived in while I was growing up, in Kumho-dong, Bongchun-dong, Shillim-dong, or Shin-dang-dong, and even in Ahyun-dong, where I'm living now. Until I entered high school, I took it for granted that the man she fawned over in the pictures was my father. I was twenty when I found out otherwise.

Just as the apple doesn't fall far from the tree, I didn't always have the best fortune. My father died before I was born, which wasn't the most fortuitous of beginnings. As a fetus in my mom's womb, I must have despaired on some level when I overheard that I'd lost my father. By the time I was born, I was already jaded. I didn't have high expectations and didn't care what happened to me, merely letting time go on its way. So if I were to tell you I once went to see a fortune-teller, I bet you'd think that was uncharacteristic of me. I honestly believed I had spirits trailing me. I have a girlfriend who was dating a married guy. She was the sneakiest, shallowest person I'd ever met. When she wanted to go see the fortune-teller, I tagged along. My mom had become inexplicably ill around that same time, so I wanted to ask about that.

When we entered the "den," the fortune-teller stared at me in a way that made me squirm uncomfortably before she announced that I had spirits all around me.

"What?" I asked incredulously.

"There are spirits behind you. You have dead people around you."

Annoyed by what I took to be her callousness, I responded calmly, "That must be my dad. He drowned."

She shook her head vehemently. And, peering at some unseen apparition behind me, she murmured, "No, that one's got torn flesh hanging from his bones. He didn't drown. He was blown up in the air."

I mentioned this to my mom over dinner. When she heard, she dropped her spoon into her soup. Then she covered her face with both hands. She stayed up all night, trembling under the covers. The next day, she brought out a photo album and turning to the first page, pointed at the sullen man in the picture. She told me he was my real father, and had recently died in a plane crash. I don't want to tell you how I felt then. I used to play classic pop songs to soothe my mom every time she got into one of her sobbing fits, but that day, as those same songs played—"Pipeline," "Chapel of Love," "I Went to Your Wedding"—it suddenly struck me why she sighed so painfully every time they played. Getting up, I walked over and turned the music off.

I refused to accept that I had another father. I'd loved another man as my father for twenty years, so I found it understandably difficult to shift paradigms. I continued to tell myself that I'd inherited my flat forehead, arched eyebrows, and optimism from my father. You think maybe he might not accept me, now that he knows I'm not his real daughter? Perhaps.

I couldn't like that man, try as I might. The fortune-teller said he was following me around, too. Why would he do that? I heard he had a child with that crafty wife of his—a boy a year younger than me—so why doesn't he follow his son around? Did he find out after death that I was his daughter?

I just had a thought. I must have three spirits following me now. My mom, the man who fathered me, and you. Even if I exclude my dad from the mix, it's a big group. I'll have to be careful when closing the door behind me. Don't worry, I'll make sure to wait until all three of you have had the chance to come inside before closing it. Wait, maybe my mom's with my dad, not me. Are ghosts bound by the laws of marriage, too?

My mom led a difficult life. For years, she cut patterns and stitched at her sister-in-law's *hanbok* shop, which allowed her to save enough money to open a small embroidery shop of her own. It soon closed. though. She worked at restaurants and sold cosmetics and sundries door to door, but nothing ever took off. She was bad at working with her hands, tired easily, was hard to get along with, and never mastered the art of white lies and empty flattery. No wonder she had so much trouble at her jobs. Other than looking pretty, there was nothing she could do. Honestly though, I liked that she was so pretty, although her being useless meant I had to do all our chores as soon as I was old enough for junior high school, including making the family *kimchi*. When she sold wares on the street from a small cloth bag, I was the one who added up the sales figures at night because she hated to calculate. The worst was when she got a restaurant job. The work was difficult, but the customers even more so. As soon as I was let out from classes at the all girls' vocational high school I attended, I dashed to the restaurant to help her, forgoing any extracurricular activities. She wasn't as hardy as I was. Her hands were always wet from doing one chore or another, leaving them cracked and blistered with pain that kept her up at night. Nightly, I smeared ointment on her fingers and followed that with a manicure. She smiled brightly as she looked down at her sad, swollen fingers, nails painted bright red. I think that's when I first thought seriously about becoming a hairstylist.

Once, she fell down a flight of stairs while struggling with a heavy cosmetics case. She broke both arms and couldn't work for two months. Meanwhile, two of her customers, young women who lived nearby, moved away without paying Mom the money they owed her. When she told me this story over heaving sobs, I marched her down to the bar where they worked. My mom couldn't bring herself to go in, so I made her wait in the alley while I set off. Once she was out of sight though, my legs began trembling.

The last work my mom did was give home facials to women. Of all her jobs, this was the most suited to her. Hosting the women who came to our home was a happy time. Mom had quite a few regulars and all her customers liked me. I steamed their towels, sliced cucumbers, and was fun to talk to and great at massages. I even offered them hair-care and styling advice, playing up my beauty school credentials. They sang my praises—"She's such a sweet little busy bee! She'll make some man very happy!"—and my mom would laugh and complain that I wasn't ladylike enough and that I'd never find a husband, as she traced arcs around the women's mouths with cream-smudged fingers, looking up at me teasingly. I remember blushing when she did that, not from embarrassment, but genuine happiness. Does happiness have to be so brief? A few months later, Mom was rushed to the hospital. She died soon after.

A few days before her death, I was shampooing her hair. She'd lost so much weight that her head felt like one of those plastic skeleton heads in elementary school science labs.

"You're good at this," she said. That was the first compliment she'd ever paid me. And the last.

I don't do it anymore, but when I was an assistant at the salon, there was a time when shampooing people's hair was all I did. Some of the male customers were shy about placing their scalp in the hands of a woman shampooer. I hear in barbershops, your hair is shampooed with your face down. But at our salon, when I told the men to lean back facing the ceiling, many of them searched anxiously with their eyes, unsure where to look. You were just as nervous when you were at my place and I offered to wash your hair. I remember your forehead crinkling at the prospect. But I succeeded in forcing you into the chair and tilting your head back. The sink came up high, and my breasts pushed against your face. Then I was the one who was embarrassed, and hurriedly covered your face with a towel. I remember the lulling sound of your even breathing escaping from the soft fabric.

On the night you died, I shampooed your hair for the second time. We'd both come home drenched from the rain.

You were the one who suggested walking in the rain. It was late and the night was quiet. Except for the rare car that passed, splashing little shiny grapes of water into the sidewalk, the street was almost empty. I wonder how many people know there are exactly 127 trees lining the street from Seo-daemun to the Ahyun subway station. We counted them slowly as we walked in the rain. Every time we came to a tree, we stopped, leaned against the wet bark, and kissed. 127 times. It was like we were leaving behind scraps of our last moments together.

Later, when I offered to wash your hair, you nodded obediently, which was surprising. You seemed tired, or maybe a little sad. Cradling your head in one arm, I began combing your hair. After running warm water over it, I lathered your hair with shampoo. Rinsing away the bubbles, I suddenly realized that I couldn't hear you breathing. Thinking you might have fallen asleep, I slowly lifted the towel. Your eyes were open, staring up at me. They were wet with tears.

"What time is it?" you asked in a faltering voice.

Smiling, I joked, "Nobody checks the time when they're happy."

Photograph 3: Your Alibi

The police came again yesterday. They asked several unimportant questions and when I gave noncommittal answers, they nodded briskly as if I'd given them a decisive clue. They told me they were ruling your death a suicide. I sat staring out the window, wishing them gone. I must have looked forlorn. One of them retrieved an old photograph from his pocket and gently beckoned for me to take a look.

It was of two women standing underneath a cherry tree. One was chubby, the other wearing a thin chain around her neck. Next to them were a boy and a girl, around six or seven years old, tiny fingers clutching the women's skirts. The girl is crying in the picture. As for the little boy? I returned the photograph to the officers without looking at his face.

"It doesn't mean anything, does it?" the one who showed me the picture asked, as he tucked it back into his pocket.

I remembered that little girl. She loved getting her picture taken. That day, she stood obediently next to her mother. A few steps away stood a man in glasses, one eye against his camera's viewfinder as he rotated the lens ring to adjust the focus. It was a bright, sunny day. While waiting for the man to take the picture, the girl noticed the black shadow he cast on the ground. It slowly twisted and turned with his every movement. Suddenly, the girl screamed. The shadow had lunged at her. She took off at a run. Shrieking, she ran as fast as she could, but her mother soon caught up with her. She ended up in the picture, with a dislocated shoulder.

You once mused about people who capture the past when the past can't serve as an alibi. You said a good alibi is solid proof of one's absence. I have a favor to ask. Prove to me you weren't in that picture. You had to have been somewhere else. That's the only way we can be innocent. Run. Run from time, run from photographs that trap you, run from our father. Run to a place where sin and time don't exist, where a dead man's curse can't destroy the living. Run to the first photograph in my mom's album. Me? I'm a lost cause. Look how I'm crying in that picture, unaware my shoulder has been pulled from its socket. I'll wait in the third picture to intercept time so it can't catch up with you. Are you on your way? Run! Run from this picture. Are you running? Are you running, my love?

What? You're gone! No!

The Age of Lyricism

I felt someone's light touch on my back. Turning, I saw no one but glimpsed a strand of hair perched gently on my shoulder. I gingerly picked it up and studied it for a long time. Age brings with it an inevitable weakening of the tensile strength of human hair. I knew it was over-sensitive to react to the loss of a single strand of hair, so I tossed it in the trash. Then I began to ponder my hypersensitivity and guilt, my anxiety, my timidity and a certain stubborn earnestness I've always had. After devoting so much energy to obsessing over my obsessive personality, I was too exhausted to focus on the actual hair loss. My mind was always filled to bursting with the analyses of a million different things but sadly, nothing that was any use in real life.

A few days later, I discovered I have female pattern baldness. When I first noticed a small patch on the crown of my head that no amount of brushing could cover, I shrugged. Only much later did I realize the patch was the size of a half-dollar. Now, I peered closely at myself in the mirror. Using both hands, I searched furiously through my hair. I can't believe it! I have a bald spot?

On the verge of tears, I quickly dialed K on the phone.

"K, this is an emergency. I have a bald spot on my head. I think it may be female pattern baldness."

K's reply was quick, as if she'd anticipated the call. "Really? You'll probably go completely bald soon. And when it rains, the rain will make plop-

82

plop-plop sounds on your head. Remember bald Mr. Park? He says that when it rains, the sound as it bounces on his head is louder than the pitter patter of raindrops on a slate roof." Then, abruptly, she asked, "By the way, did you have lunch yet?"

"No," I bleated weakly.

"There's this new place near my work that makes excellent stir-fried octopus, and they have an incredible chili sauce."

"…So?"

"So come out and buy me lunch."

This was her way of reassuring me—cool, arrogant. But being the literal-minded person I was, I had trouble accepting this kind of "help."

"I'm facing a serious problem, and all you can say is let's meet for lunch? Are you even human?" I barked into the phone.

"Of course I'm human. How can anything be more human than hunger? Even Ulysses went out to eat after his men died. He only began to mourn them after he was full. Shouldn't you be more sensitive to this stuff? You're a writer, for Christ's sake."

Well aware that my proclivity to take offense at the smallest things stemmed from my eagerness to please, K added, "Isn't it time for you to stop getting so emotional over everything?"

I developed my serious nature at the age of six—which is as far back as memory allows me to go—when I awakened one morning to find I was no longer being treated as a child. The day before, I was just a snot-nosed little girl. I naturally assumed this would carry over to the next day, so I stayed in bed, even after the rest of my family had cleared the breakfast table. But unlike the day before, my parents didn't wake me, nor, curiously, did they yell at me to get up.

"Is she still in bed?" my father asked, chewing his breakfast.

"Let her be. She's starting school next year so she's old enough to take care of herself now," my mother replied.

This conversation jolted me awake. I didn't open my eyes, but I was shocked nevertheless. So this is how you become a grownup. Suddenly, without warning.

No one chided me for spilling food on the table or ordered me back to the sink to wash my neck because it wasn't clean enough. At the end of every conversation, my parents would offhandedly remark, "Oh, right, you're an adult now," which effectively stripped me of my right to be uninhibited, as children are. Unaware that this was a tactic grownups use to trick children into growing up sooner than they'd like, I felt desperately guilty every time they reminded me of my premature maturity. After all, I still thought of myself as a kid. How naïve of my parents to overestimate me.

I began carrying myself in a safe, prudish manner. I swore to behave as an adult so I wouldn't let my trusting parents down. I began to think and speak as an adult. I tried hard to believe that life wasn't what I thought it was cut out to be.

Because I was a year younger than the recommended starting age for first graders, and since my birthday fell at the end of October, I wasn't supposed to start elementary school that year. Only after my dad had pulled some strings could I march along with the rest of the schoolchildren as they huffed and puffed across the soccer field to get to class. As a result, I remained perpetually one year younger than my classmates. I never got sick, didn't get held back, and didn't have to go into the army, either, so when I applied to my university's doctoral program (unsuccessfully), I was only twenty-four years old. I never doubted my precociousness and freely divulged this trait to everyone I met. No one guessed the gaping, embarrassing emptiness that I carried around inside me like the empty patch on the crown of my head.

My dad was equal parts eloquent, silent, and blistering with his tongue when he wanted to be. When he was little, he climbed a utility pole and cut several wires, shrouding the entire town in darkness—all for the sake of a science experiment. Later, he put this creativity and pioneering spirit into business, once placing a thatched roof atop a two-story building. Starting with nothing, his innovative ideas and hard work allowed him to become a masterful entrepreneur and to achieve success as a local developer. Photographs of him proudly receiving awards from the town council for things like paving streets and building the new police station appeared not infrequently in the local paper and on the council's bulletin board. Given his line of work, he was often "contracted" to do "jobs," terminology with a decidedly gangster-film feel to them. Despite that, my dad also strummed folk songs on his guitar, crooned "Love Is a Many Splendored Thing" and "Sad Movie," and could even play the drums passably. He kept measuring equipment, blueprints, and T-squares on his desk. Thanks to him, our family became the first in town to own a TV.

Although a busy man, he aimed to be a cool, attentive dad. He never shouted at me. He didn't pressure me to study, either, save to often remind me how in six years in elementary school he never got an answer wrong on a test except one time in first grade spelling when he confused "roast chestnuts" with "roasted chestnuts." He always ended our conversations with praise and little pearls of wisdom, such as "you're my pride and joy," "we live by pride and pride alone," "learn to be humble," which confirmed to me that I was being treated as an equal.

The year I turned nine, my dad bought cheap land on the outskirts of town and built a modern two-story house. In a poor village swarming with naked children, where thatched-roof huts clustered around the town's spirit tree, the house was a marvel. Believing that children must grow up greeting the sun as it rose, Dad installed southeast-facing windows in our room, as well as a modern kitchen and a basement. He planted seventy rosebushes in the yard and planned to build a large study and family rec room on the second floor. The neighborhood kids assumed we were rich when they saw trucks delivering sand to our property and hydraulic cutters churning out rebar like noodles.

My mom and grandmother, however, were skeptical of Dad's promises, believing half of what he said was baloney. Many times, we made plans for a picnic and sat waiting eagerly for dad to come home, only to resign ourselves to the fact he wasn't coming and settle down to a dinner of cold picnic food. Once, when we did go on a trip to a nearby river, our dad barked at us to gather underneath a tree so he could take pictures of us, prompting grandma to mutter, "Funny how I always see him with a camera but never see the photos." I felt no one but me truly appreciated Dad and how much he was doing for us.

The modern house never really came to fruition, even after five years, which was when we left town. On the surface, it looked like a respectable two-story home, but the house was sadly deficient on the inside, with only three rooms and a half-completed kitchen on the first floor. I tried to be understanding. What wasn't there to understand? Dad's business went bankrupt. He couldn't help that. Nothing in life goes according to plan.

Once, I received an award from UNESCO, an organization whose exotic name suggested serious, purposeful work. I came in second place in an essay contest titled "UNESCO Hosts: The International Children's Art Exhibition." We were to submit essays on the exhibition, which I didn't get to visit. I wrote mine based on the abstract details offered by our art teacher, who

had seen the exhibition. When she received the call from UNESCO inform-
ing her she was to bring me to the host city for the awards ceremony, she
was thrilled. I didn't find it odd that the grownups praised me for polishing
our school's reputation rather than admonishing me for lying my way into
winning a contest. And I wasn't disappointed because I considered myself
one of them. Feeling excited, as if I were privy to a conspiracy, I went a step
further and justified my actions: *All writing can be considered fiction.*

My maturity took me to nether places in the adult world. On the day
we learned about the essay contest win, my dad was so pleased he took my
art teacher, vice-principal, and me to one of the "teahouses" he frequented
back in those days. Several female "entertainers" greeted us at the door and
escorted us inside. Dad had trouble remembering the name of the girl next
to him. One too many times, he turned to her and wondered, "Sweetie, what
was your name again? Chung? Jang?" Finally, I blurted, "Dad, it's Ms. Jang!"
Everyone burst out laughing. I didn't notice that my dad and teacher were
laughing a little too loud, maybe out of guilt for bringing a child to what
was effectively a hostess bar. I was merely proud to be included in their midst,
laughing mightily with the rest of them.

I had my fair share of trials, too. My grandmother, who took over the
child-rearing responsibilities when my parents became too busy with the
business, began coughing up green gunk every day and finally succumbed to
cancer, and my brother ran away from home. Then a bunch of men kicked
our door down one morning and slapped red repo stickers on our armoire,
our TV—on anything of value, really. I waited for Dad to come sailing in
on his motorcycle, the way he always did, reach inside his leather bomber
jacket, and hand us a brick of cash wrapped in newspaper, but he didn't
come.

When we left town—which we did in a hurry in the middle of the
night—with Dad still away in another town and Mom sick and wheezing, I
was only fifteen years old, a precarious age that could have left me dumb
with sorrow or furious with teen angst. Instead, I remained as serious as ever.
Ignoring the very real, concrete problems before me, I chose to wax philo-
sophical on themes like human solitude, the soul, the sophisticated theta,
and the like. Plodding diligently through Sartre, Carl Hilty, and Thomas
Wolfe, I was struck by the vulgar realization that none of them were as en-
tertaining as my favorite bestselling author. Ashamed, I quickly spent my al-
lowance on a massive anthology of the Classics, then sighed and basked in

the elitist awareness that I was dedicating my life to pursuing matters of the intellect. Obviously, many of my classmates found me funny/disgusting. I now consider the old me disgusting. At the time though, I coolly ignored the pointed stares of my peers and chose to look toward the far horizon.

My earnestness blinded me to reality, and my conservative side placed a wall around me. I believed I was smart, sophisticated, and even, to a degree, crafty. I suffered the guilt of knowingly obscuring my corruption. For a while, I went to church and prayed. Then, one bitterly cold winter morning, I moved into the third floor of a dorm and began life in Seoul as a college student at a women's university.

The hair loss was getting worse. What started out as a quarter-sized spot expanded into a patch the size of a mason jar lid. They say one shouldn't count their beauty marks, or more of them will appear; maybe I spent too much time peering at my head.

The Patch has already caused discomfort on numerous occasions. Once, over drinks with friends, I snorted and loudly cursed the superficiality of life before lowering my head to sip my drink. Suddenly, I realized my audience had a full view of the Patch. Embarrassed, I quickly sat back up. I felt self-conscious speaking about my dedication to pure literature when it felt like the Patch was mocking my words. I was careful at meet-the-author events. Sometimes, I caught myself laughing at TV comedians doing a skit about hobos until I saw the fake bald patches they were wearing on their heads. Furtively, I stole glances at my family to see if they'd noticed the similarity. The worst was when I caught myself laughing at myself. I felt manifestly pathetic.

I called K again.

"I got a call from a guy I went to college with," I told K.

"Why'd he call?"

"He reads my column and said I've done some good pieces. We agreed to meet next week."

"What for?"

"I wanted to see him."

"That's weird."

"Oh, and I'm going to be out of town attending a wake. I'm worried about the Patch."

"Who cares? People will just think they're seeing the reflection of the moon across Lake Geneva."

"I'm serious. Do you think I should go?"

"No one's going to be looking at your head."

"There will be some guys there I'd like to look nice for. I can't do that when I'm bald."

"That's true. I don't think you could pull that off. So don't go."

"I have to. It would be rude not to go."

"So go."

"I want to, but I'm self-conscious about my hair!"

"What's the problem? Either you go, or you don't go. Simple as that. I'm busy. I have to go."

"You're brushing this off because it's not your problem."

"No, I said I'm busy. Why are you being childish?"

"You're so mean."

"I'm mean?"

"No, you're not mean. You're great!"

I was about to hang up when I heard K's voice again. Putting the phone against my ear, I heard K suggesting, "If you're that worried, go see a hair-stylist."

I snapped, "I'm busy!" I didn't mention I was at a hair salon.

A hairstylist approached and began spraying water on my hair. Suddenly, she recoiled.

"Oh, you have that female pattern baldness thing!"

I replied levelly, "Yes. I've had it for a while. Seems my hair and I aren't on the same team anymore."

"We have several customers who have this. Have you been to a derma-tologist?"

"I planned to, but couldn't find the time."

"What do you mean, couldn't find the time? Proper hair and skincare is everything to a woman!" she exclaimed dramatically. After a few more pooh-poohs, she began blow-drying my hair. "How do you want it? I guess you want me to cover it up?"

Squinting, she gasped, "Oh, it's much bigger than I thought! Ma'am, you need to see a doctor soon. This will get worse if you don't do some-thing."

Feeling like I should say something to ease her concern, I reassured her. "I can use hairpins to strategically cover it up."

After she finished, she brought a can of hairspray. I worried that it might stiffen my hair and make the Patch more conspicuous. When I carefully voiced my opinion, the hairstylist declared, "Absolutely not! This will hold the hair in place."

Not wanting to betray her good intentions, I meekly obeyed.

I arrived at the downtown meeting spot, where a bus was waiting to take us to the wake. A few people loitering outside recognized me and waved. Thankfully, they didn't seem to notice the Patch. Climbing in, I immediately scuttled to a window seat on the left side of the bus, fearing that any other seat would draw attention to the Patch, which was on the left side of my head. I didn't want anyone to see it. But just as I was about to sit down, A, considerate friend that he is, knowingly beckoned me over.

"Let me take a look," he whispered. "My wife had this, too, but it soon got better."

A part of me wanted to reach up and hide the offending spot, but I feared that doing so would admit it as a flaw. Instead, I chirped cheerfully, "Oh? So it's curable. That's a relief!"

I turned my face toward the window so A wouldn't see the flush on my cheeks.

When B sat down next to me, I told her about the Patch. I decided it was better to come out guns blazing than to cower in a corner. B crinkled her forehead and murmured worriedly, "Is it painful?"

I laughed. "It'll no doubt get better!" Underneath my shirt, a single bead of sweat rolled from my armpit all the way down to my waist. I should have refused the hairspray. The hairstylist wouldn't have minded if I'd put up a fight.

Somehow, I was reminded of my mom. Whenever she came to Seoul, she made it a point to call all her friends.

"Darling! I just arrived in the big city. You're the first one I'm calling! I wanted to call from the bus terminal but didn't have change or a calling card. All the shops selling the cards were closed, too. I wanted to buy a drink and use the change to call you, but my daughter, who'd come to pick me up in her car, complained that we were wasting too much time when parking's so expensive. I called as soon as I got here, with the shoes still on my feet!"

Be it her third day or tenth day in the city, that's the story she always told her girlfriends, be they Friend 1, Friend 2, Friend 3, etc. Fed up with her lies, I'd yell, "Mom, what's the big deal? Why do you lie to them? Your friends won't mind that they weren't the first person you called. It's not like they sit by the phone all day waiting to hear your voice."

Still, she made the same phone calls. I caught myself wanting to scream at her and realized this was a flaw of mine. I'm not forgiving of other people's behavior. I smiled bitterly to myself. I'm a lot like my mom.

By the time the bus pulled up to the wake, it was already dark. After paying my respects, I sat down at a table where dinner and drinks were to be served. I braced myself. I have to behave myself tonight. I can't be the all-knowing cosmopolitan. I can't leave these folks with a lasting impression of an obnoxious bald woman lifting her glass for a drunken toast. I sat next to B, the only other female there, and in my head, practiced saying the words, 'I'm sorry, but I rarely drink. I'll take one glass, but that's it.'

Just then, someone came over from the next table and offered me a drink.

"Hi. I'm X. I live in Jeonju," he introduced himself.

"Oh, hello!" I replied, pleased. "I went to high school in Jeonju." I never went to any of the reunions, but I was proud of my alma mater. I didn't like choosing sides based on hometowns or high schools, but in my eagerness to please, I tried to be agreeable.

"Really? I went to high school there, too, Class of '52."

"I'm a graduate of the all girls' school, Class '48."

We struck up a conversation. It would have been rude to refuse his drinks, and it worried me that he might think I was playing coy. In second grade, my homeroom teacher described me as "mild-mannered and very ladylike." I was already a lady at eight years old. Along with being described as "mature," being called "ladylike" gave me gravitas. I accepted the drinks.

Pretty soon, I forgot about the Patch. When the conversation turned to life, literature, and love, I offered my two cents' worth. I was quite vocal on the issue of celebrities' looks.

"You think C is handsome? Really?" I guffawed. "He's not handsome! Girls fall for him, sure, but not all girls are the same. Some girls fall for smart, worldly authority figures. Then you have other, wiser girls who can't bear the fact they're getting old and as a result, chase good-looking, younger men. If C were a simple guy, he'd be sleeping around all the time and generally living a satisfying, peaceful life. But his story's way more complicated than that. He's vain enough to know girls adore him but smart enough not to let that define who he is. In fact, it would offend him to be accused of being otherwise. C probably feels uncomfortable about his good looks when he's with

90

people to whom physical beauty doesn't matter. What's ironic is that although he knows the screaming girls haven't got one brain among them and that they're only in love with the idea of him, deep inside, he's lonely. Who can blame him? After all, we're all incomplete. Everyone has weaknesses and flaws. I'm a fan of C, too. I must be a girl at heart. Wait, am I the only one talking?"

More drinks were offered my way. The more I drank, the more I believed everyone was being nice. Little did I know they were fighting back tears of laughter as the Patch bobbed up and down while I proselytized. It was a good night.

It took me a long time to grow up. Even at nineteen, I knew nothing.

My first night in the dorm, I followed one of the sophomores to the cafeteria and ate off a tray for the first time in my life.

"Look at these scrawny yards. What little wimpy ribbons they are," she complained, picking at a dish of cooked scallions. What we called green onions, she described as "yard onions" in her strange northern accent. *Everything here is so different*, I thought to myself. I had to learn everything from scratch. I took in a deep breath, trying to collect and steel myself at the same time. Another sophomore sauntered by. Sitting next to me, she grinned.

"Is this the new fish?" she asked the girl who'd brought me.

"Yeah. She looks like a nice kid, doesn't she?" my sophomore replied loyally.

"Yeah. It's obvious she's a freshman. Some of us want to set the first years up on a group blind date, but she looks like she's twelve years old."

Blushing, I removed the clip in my hair. The new girl advised me to get my hair permed and wear heels to the date if I didn't want the boys to "take me for a fool." Only after she left did I stick the clip back. I thought I looked cuter with it than without. On the day of the much ballyhooed group date, I fished it out of my pocket and quickly clipped it in before walking into the bar.

The boy assigned to me had on a black shirt open at the collar. He was a Seoul kid, and when I walked in, was lazily sprawled in a corner, smoking. He had a clean, white face, talked like Camus, looked like a rebel, and explained that he'd taken a semester off while in high school to form a band. Even when he was studying to get into college, he often skipped class to look at drums at the downtown music shops. He was only two years older than me but I sensed an enormous depth of life in his cynical tone.

"Yesterday, I was lying on the grass in one of our school's lawns and decided not to go to class," he said.

"Why?" I whispered.

"The sky was just too blue."

I swallowed hard. The only complaint I had with college was that no one told me what I had to do. I wished we had morning assembly like we did in high school. To meet someone who found lectures dull was shocking.

I was a good listener. When he told me about his break-up with his high school girlfriend, I tried damn hard to get him to see my maturity, my intellectual breadth. Anxiously hoping he'd take me out again, I gave a noncommittal "Sure, I guess" when he asked if he could call me the next day. Underneath the table, my hands were shaking. When he passed me a piece of paper with his number on it, I had to wipe my clammy hands on my jeans before accepting it.

Our next date was scheduled for a week later. I waited for him in a hooded sweater with a rabbit on the front, the trusty clip in my hair. Thirty minutes passed, with no him. When he showed up, almost an hour late, he apologized and explained that he'd been forced to go to another group date. Nodding in sympathy, I told him it was okay, that I took it to mean he enjoyed our group date so much he had to go to this one, too, which meant he really liked me. At that, he laughed. Proud of myself, I laughed with him.

I found his dark personality hard to take. He made daily threats to leave school and muttered that he should be playing drums at some small, anonymous club out of town. His face grew paler by the day. Even setting aside Deep Purple's "Soldier of Fortune," which he had on repeat every night in his room, his favorite tracks were all depressingly dreary—"Epitaph," "Ace of Sorrow." I couldn't understand why he didn't try to find joy and meaning through me. Certain I was his salvation, it was disappointing to me that he didn't see what I saw.

One of the reasons dorm life never gets boring is because you never run out of people to talk about. Who's the prettiest freshman? Who's the prettiest sophomore? Who has the most complicated love life? Who has a different boy bringing her home every night, right before the clock strikes the nine o'clock curfew? One of the freshmen, Hye-ran, was known as being fashionable, fearless, and frivolous. When she spotted me walking with the pale guy, she decided he was hot enough that she'd deign to go out with one of his friends if I could arrange a double date. I thought this might improve his mood, so I agreed.

On the day of our date, Hye-ran showed up in big hoop earrings, a plunging V-neck, and a chic scarf. She matched the racy shirt with flashy bell bottoms. Her sleeves were covered in patchwork denim. Nervously, I fingered the pink ribbon on my blouse, but told myself I had no reason to fear a girl so obviously shallow. We sat at a table illuminated by a red light. I ordered orange juice, as I always did, but Hye-ran asked for a glass of sweet red wine. She had an air of imperious sophistication about her. She steered the conversation toward topics such as relationships, and peppered her speech with sultry laughter. The two guys ate it up. The only time they looked my way was when we clinked glasses for the occasional toast.

On her suggestion, we began to arm wrestle. Hye-ran began whimpering as soon as she and her date began and quickly surrendered. When it was my turn, I threw my weight against my partner's hand, veins popping in my neck. Seeing how eagerly I wanted to win, my guy loosened his grip, giving me the victory. But nobody seemed to cheer my win. Instead, I sensed them trying to fight back laughter.

After that, I leaned back in my chair and stayed sullenly quiet. Glancing my way, he asked, "Are you bored? Want to play with matchsticks?"

Happy that he was finally paying attention to me (I knew he still liked me!), I leaned forward and studied his long, white fingers as they worked to build something with the matchsticks. He failed each time. Unable to guess what he was trying to build, I leaned closer, hoping to impress him with my undivided attention. In the end, frustrated, he threw the matches and yelled, "Will you move your head? You're breathing so hard the sticks can't stay up!"

We were nearing curfew, so we left the restaurant. Passing by a small snack bar, he suggested we grab a quick bite, since we were still hungry. Hye-ran ordered four fried tofu noodle bowls without asking if that was what we all wanted. I was wiping my mouth after I'd finished my bowl when Hye-ran's guy pointed at my mouth and teased, "You have a big pepper flake stuck in your teeth. You should check a mirror."

I felt a wave of panic. Hye-ran giggled, "It's true! Want to borrow my mirror?"

In a low voice, I said, "There's no pepper flake."

"How do you know?" She was about to die laughing.

Pointing at the bowl of noodles, I sputtered, "There were no flakes in

93

the noodles. How could I have one in my teeth?"

At that, the three erupted in laughter.

"You're smart, girl!" Hye-ran managed through her tears. The pale guy said something in agreement, but it was drowned in laughter.

Despite that, I knew I still retained my trusty redeeming quality: my ability to understand everything, even, I believed, men. A few days after the double date, I finally succeeded in convincing myself that he wasn't laughing at me. He couldn't have been. Last month, he'd stopped by his house to change so he could take the train with me to Jeonju, where my parents still lived, although he ended up not going because there were no train tickets left. And what about all the nice places he took me to? The pretty coffee shops? He even gave me a tape mix! He was always so sweet. He was definitely going to call. I knew it.

I waited a month for him to call. Somewhere, I heard freshmen guys had to shave their heads for their mandatory basic army training. I was certain he was avoiding me because he was embarrassed about his new haircut. *He'll call after he grows it out,* I thought. But he didn't call. One day, I realized it was now three months into the semester, and I'd experienced a heartbreak so great I didn't grasp how bad it was.

I didn't have time to nurse my wounds because I soon became very busy. After joining the school newspaper, I aligned myself with the movement calling for the ouster of the university president. I sat with other people on the campus lawn to discuss how writing fiction in this disturbing day and age was a shameless luxury. I became engrossed in a study group on the Social History of Literature and the Arts. Then I became engrossed in planning ways to leave the group. And throughout it all, I found time for more group dates.

That autumn, however, I let my earnestness unfurl and set sail toward another relationship. I met him in a book club whose membership consisted of kids from my hometown. He was the object of all the girls' affection and knew it. First disgusted, then fascinated, I was drawn to him. He had a list of things he looked for in a woman: "One, a cheerful personality; two, honesty; three, humility..." At that, I exclaimed out loud, "Wait, that's me!" He looked up and straight into my eyes, shocked by my daring. That's when he first noticed me. Not long after, we began secretly dating. It was kept secret because he wanted it that way. He told me he'd already gotten in trouble once during high school because of a girl, due to his hopelessly handsome

94

looks and sharp intellect. He didn't want the same thing to happen in college.

After we saw the movie "One Flew Over the Cuckoo's Nest," he waxed philosophically on the issues of mankind and freedom as we sat on a bench in one of Seoul's old palaces. He described the origin of commonly used words such as "unprecedented" and explained why famed Chinese mastermind Zhuge Liang had no choice but to punish his devoted subject. He seemed deeply moved by his own words. I was amazed to learn that he wrote novels in high school. He was a man of many gifts. But despite the connection I felt we had, the next day, I was completely ignored. I had to force myself not to look at him as I argued my points at the book club.

I was exasperated by his ambiguous behavior. I wanted to mean something to him and wanted the world to see it. It didn't help when one of the girls from the book club tearfully asked me for advice on how to get closer to him—the man I worshipped.

Despite rumors about his affairs, he didn't seem too keen or eager to win any woman's heart. He was rather aloof. When we met, we usually sat in one place for hours. I often had to massage the circulation back into my legs to walk again. He called me regularly, was punctual and sweet, but something was missing. This was my first big romance, but it lacked real panache and passion. All we did was go to the movies, drink tea, and go home. Once, I summoned the courage to tell him, "I don't know whether you see me as just another girl from the book club, as a friend, or as a girlfriend."

As if answering a question on a survey, he responded, "I'd say it's the third option."

Seeing each other twice a week didn't bring us any closer, so when we went two weeks before our next date, the awkwardness was unbearable. He tried to say something, but the music at the coffee shop drowned him out. Ironically, the song playing over the speakers was "Speak with the Eyes." I told him this.

"What did you say?" he shouted. "I can't hear you!"

"I said, this is 'Speak with the Eyes'!"

"What?"

"This song! It's called 'Speak with the Eyes'!"

"What?"

"Can you hear me?"

"No, I can't hear you!"

After a short silence, I tried again, being the more persevering of the two. "How have you been?"

He didn't reply. "This place is fucking noisy," he muttered, glaring at his cup.

We were both quiet after that. Soon, we got up and left. I was getting tired of dealing with his edge. He was quiet as we chewed fried pork cutlets at a small restaurant. When the waiter took away the plates, he lit a cigarette. Solemnly, he spoke, "Thank you for everything."

"Spring, Summer, Winter and Fall" was playing on the radio. He went on to say that the future might bring us together again by chance, just as chance brought us together this time. Those words were just beautiful enough to make me forgive him. Wanting to prove I was big enough to let idle matters—like getting dumped by an emotionally-unavailable man—slide, I talked with greater animation, guessing the titles of the songs on the radio, and even counting the stars in the night sky as he walked me to my dorm. That night, I stayed up watching a movie, "Autumn Returns," with my roommate, crying into my pillow.

I'd lost the will to live. For three days, I stayed buried under the covers, listening to "The Saddest Thing" and "The End of the World." At times, I dragged myself to the window and muttered out loud at the birds chirping outside, *Don't they know the world's ended? Why are they singing?* Three days later, I received a letter from him. He wrote that, after our breakup, he'd tried in vain to get drunk and that the wind from the river no longer felt cool and refreshing. We got back together, and grew closer. We even held hands at the park near our dormitory building. That night, I wrote in my journal:

> His face looked empty as he leaned against the wind. He brought a cigarette to his lips. I like the sight of a man lighting a cigarette. When he cups his hands close to his face to protect the flame against the wind, I think his is the most beautiful face in the world. He tossed the still-lit matchstick on the ground. When I told him I feel betrayed when men carelessly throw away their matchsticks once they've served their purpose, he laughed. We leaned our bodies on the swings and looked up at the sky as he smoked. For the time it took for the cigarette to turn to ash, we observed each other as two stars might. I felt happy. Rubbing out the cigarette, he said we should leave. I was about to agree, but I froze. He'd reached out and grabbed my hand. That's when I re-

alized the hand is the most sensitive body part we have.

If I were being honest, I'd have said hands are superfluous and uncomfortable. I wrote what I did because I thought it made me sound smart, but the holding of hands felt so awkward I strode as quickly as I could to the dorm. As he was taking those long drags of his cigarette, he must have been debating the best way to hold my hand.

Our relationship didn't last. Come winter, we saw more of each other without progressing beyond hand holding. Our routine went something like this: He'd call and ask if he could see me tomorrow. I'd hesitate before saying yes. He'd tell me not to worry if tomorrow were a bad time, we could always reschedule. I'd reassure him that tomorrow's fine. He'd make it a date, then hang up. Once I was sure the line was dead, I'd scream into the phone. *Why would it be a bad time? If it were a bad time, I would have said it was a bad time!*

We were walking outside Seoul Station one snowy night. The road was iced over, and I'd already slipped several times. Gritting my teeth, I did my best to keep my dignity, but once, I almost fell flat on my butt, righting myself just in time. After about twenty minutes, he finally offered, "Um, if it's all right with you, you can hold my arm."

Delirious from our newfound intimacy, he took me to a department store that evening and bought me a pair of fur-lined gloves. We looked so awkward that the sales clerk giggled the entire time she was wrapping the gloves. I wore the gloves all winter long.

When classes let out for winter break, we went to our hometown and picked up where we left off. We had a set route for our walks—past the Joy Inn and in front of Blessing Church with its two neon-red crosses capping the steeple. Usually, we stayed about two feet from each other, fearful someone we knew might see us. Wherever the lighting was dim, we held hands. On the day we decided to drop the honorifics in addressing one another, we stayed silent for so long that a passing stranger would have figured we were in a fight. We could have gotten much closer that winter if it weren't for that fateful day, December 31, when I reverted to my old, formal self.

Park benches lose all their romance in the winter, especially when they're next to a pond, inviting the cold, harsh wind from all directions. We were the only ones shivering on a bench on December 31, when most people were out merrymaking at parties and downtown bars. Christmas lights were strung around a pagoda overlooking the pond, but instead of looking festive, they seemed sad. Yet I didn't want to leave.

I probably yammered on and on about stars and ponds and the significance of another year's passing. I was so involved in my own talk that I didn't notice he'd been quiet for a long time. Finally, I turned to face him. I was surprised to see he was looking at me.

"What's wrong?" I asked, then froze.

He brought one hand slowly to my cheek. My body immediately tensed up. Out of nowhere, however, I remembered my role as savior. I must not lose my dignity. I shouldn't become like one of those other girls. I can't show him I'm nervous about my first kiss. Willing my voice to stay stern, I admonished, "Will you be able to look at me after this?"

I wasn't saying no to the kiss. I merely wanted to hide the fact that I was a jittery ball of nerves. That's why when he gasped and hurriedly turned away, I was confused.

After that, we broke up. One day, I realized I hadn't heard from him in a month. I accepted that it was over, not knowing why it ended. I guessed it had something to do with the fact we were both old-fashioned, too grim, and too proud to make any decisive moves. I did have my regrets. I felt stupid for ruining my very first kiss by putting on airs to hide my vulnerability.

Another semester began. I was a sophomore, and a busy one at that. I had to catch my favorite cartoon on Mondays at six o'clock. I had student protests to participate in at city hall. I had school festivals to attend. I had choir rehearsals. I had a secret crush to nurse. I went on volunteering trips where I helped build embankments in rural towns. I learned to play the guitar from a teacher with two missing fingers. I went shopping for lip gloss and silk blouses. I took French classes and memorized words from "Vocabulary 2000." Together with six friends from the Korean language department, I wrote poetry and even published two volumes. I won prizes we awarded to one another. I had movies to see—*Rocky, Papillon, Las Minez,* and *Drunken Master*—as well as plays to catch—*Equus* and *Pig Dreams*. I got caught purchasing a banned copy of *Realism in Our Times* and had to attend a lesson on forbidden books. I had to go night fishing with my family. I watched the trial for civil rights activist and later president Kim Dae-jung. I took trips to the East Sea, Busan, and Jeju Island. I sang songs by popular singer-songwriters. I took classes at the Beachside Poets' Academy. I went out for beers on days the campus was closed. I spent an entire summer finishing assignments at the county library. When I finally came up to breathe, I realized I was graduating soon.

Several times, I ran into the guy I almost kissed. He came to see me before going into the army. He asked, "Did you think I wouldn't need you? You were wrong."

I didn't say anything. I was analyzing his tone of voice and determining that it still didn't carry enough emotion for me to trust him. I didn't call the number he gave me. I decided what we had should be cherished as a fond memory, nothing more.

A few years later, I saw him again, outside the public restrooms at Seoul Station. I was sending off a boyfriend who was leaving on a business trip. While waiting for him outside the men's room, I heard someone call my name. "Is it you?"

I turned around, and there he was. I thought these things only happened in pop songs. I couldn't believe he was there. My heart leaped to my throat. I prayed my boyfriend would take his time in the men's room, or better yet, never come out. Grinning, he said, "Let me use the restroom first, then we can catch up."

And then, as if in a movie, he walked inside just as my boyfriend emerged. Their shoulders brushed one another. When he came back outside, he was shocked to find me standing next to another man. Clumsily, I introduced them to one another. He nodded politely, then, bidding farewell, got lost in the crowd. I stared after him until he disappeared. Although I was there to see my boyfriend off on a two-day business trip, the incident left me feeling inexplicably helpless and frustrated. I took it out on the boyfriend, who finally blew up at me. When he came back the next day, I had to beg him to forgive me.

Many years have passed. Twenty years ago we shared that winter together. Sometimes, I thought of him, especially when I chanced upon handsome men in trench coats, or when someone asked me about the first man I ever loved. I thought of him when life brought me down, when I felt terribly old and broken and lonely. Whenever I heard the phrase, "memory of a first kiss," I thought of him and wondered if we'd still be together if I hadn't ruined that kiss.

Next thing I knew, I was old enough to go to a casual meeting with a guy for no better reason than that we were members of the same club in college. We hadn't seen each other in ten years and I had the Patch to worry about. Nevertheless, I found myself waiting for him at the place we'd agreed to meet. Suddenly, I realized this guy was close friends with the first man I loved.

Soon, he showed up. He still had his babyish features. In college, he came off a little too quiet, bordering on cynical, but age had softened him quite a bit. His voice sounded cheery as he greeted me, "Wow, you haven't aged one bit! You've never looked better!"

"What are you talking about? I'm an old hag," I countered. "You have no idea how many wrinkles I have. I look young only because I dress the part. I'd look old if I walked around in a business suit, believe me. I honestly think the only reason I look young is because I don't look good in suits, being short and all. That's why I have to dress casually, which helps me look young! And what do you mean I've never looked better? Are you serious? Well, if you meant that I'm carrying myself better, I'd agree with you there. Now that I have a job I consider to be my calling in life, I definitely have a lot more confidence. I don't care as much what people think about me, and I'm smiling a lot more. I definitely have more energy about me."

I clamped my mouth shut. He was only offering a greeting. I didn't have to start analyzing and defending myself like that. If it had been K, she'd have brushed off his comment with a short, "However old we are is the new twenty!" or "Everyone's getting younger except me!" I'm not completely un-practiced in offering quick, witty banter, but when I get the slightest bit nervous, I retreat to my old, defensive position and come out swinging.

He and I had lunch and went out to tea. I kept cracking jokes to make up for the bad first impression. We started discussing bygone days.

"What happened to D?" I asked. "I remember he had a thing for E."

"Ah, D. He wrote E a letter every single day when he was in the army. He didn't win her back but his handwriting improved so much. I heard he had a comfortable time of it in the army. What happened to F?"

"Oh, her..."

"And G?"

"Him?"

After ticking off the names, a tense hesitation fell over us. We'd come to the the first guy I loved, the near-miss kiss.

"He was living abroad, but I heard he recently came back to Korea," my friend began. "He has a good job and lives in a big apartment in Gangnam, so I guess you can say he made it."

"Who did he marry?"

"He always liked those sophisticated, sexy types."

Really? That's strange, I thought to myself. I'd assumed the total opposite. I thought he liked quiet, conservative girls.

"In any case, he's the type of guy who maps out his life ahead of time, so he married a woman who could help him reach his goals," he went on. "His wife is smart and beautiful. And successful, too."

"I see," I nodded. After a moment of hesitation, I decided to lay it all out. "Did you know he and I were sort of close?"

He grinned. He obviously had a lot to say on the issue.

"Of course I did. I gave him a lot of advice, too. He wasn't sure what to do. I mean, you were sweet and cute and all, but he had another plan for himself. I mean, you're not exactly drop dead gorgeous, and you didn't go to the best schools. Your family isn't that successful, either. Besides, you were a language major. You weren't on track to becoming a doctor or anything. He didn't think you were right for his plan. He didn't consider you were marriage material. He liked you, sure, so he kept seeing you, but later, he told me he broke up with you because he didn't want to get in way over his head. Who knew you were going to become a famous writer?"

In college, I strove to be his savior, to rescue him from his unhappiness. But he wasn't a lost soul in need of salvation. It turns out what he wanted was a woman who could offer him real, more material support.

At nineteen years old, I was so caught up in my own solemn sense of purpose that the pain of a breakup simply didn't compute. Only now, twenty years later, did I realize how massively, how thoroughly I'd been dumped for another girl.

For someone whose carefully guarded love has been just ripped up and trampled on, I was unexpectedly calm. "I see. Here I was thinking he was a helpless guy."

I started to laugh. Inside, I thought, *So this is how it goes. I'm not surprised at all. That's life.* After that, as my friend continued to reminisce, I let my thoughts wander and spun a cheap, predictable soap opera plot: Unable to rid himself of the ugly, helpless girl who loves him, he searches for ways to escape her clutches. Meanwhile, blind to his true intentions, she continues to believe she can rescue him.

As soon as I got home, I turned on my laptop and typed a title for a new story, "First Love."

Suddenly, I thought of the guy who enjoyed listening to "Soldier of Fortune." Where he is now? What's he up to? Is he still skinny? Does he still wear black shirts? Does he still smoke? Did he form a band? I frowned.

Wait, am I getting the two guys mixed up? Was he the man I first loved, and not the guy I almost kissed? There was nothing to stop me from reinterpreting my past. An alternate perspective would result in a different story.

I got up to go to the bathroom. Washing my hands, I looked up to see my face in the mirror. The Patch was right in my line of sight. I didn't even have to brush my hair back. I took a step closer and stared at the bald spot for a long time.

I returned to my computer but my interest in the story had already evaporated. Lost in thought, I typed half-heartedly. Everyone has a weakness. Some weaknesses are ridiculous, like a bald patch, or a skipped adolescence.

I called K. "Are you busy? Can you talk?"

"You sound nice today. What happened? I've got time. What's up?"

"Nothing much. Remember I told you I was meeting that guy from college?"

"Yeah."

"We met today."

"Yeah?"

"I don't know why I used to be so immature."

"What do you mean?"

"I had no idea everyone was laughing at me. I took everything so seriously."

"..."

"I was such a fool," I continued.

"And you think you've changed?"

"Now my problem is that I hide my feelings so well. I try really hard to stay on guard and not let it show that I'm such a moron."

"If you say so."

I didn't like K's tone. She was being too... nice. My voice grew louder. "Fine. To be honest, I know I looked pathetic twenty years ago when I took everything so seriously, and I know I still take things seriously. The thing is, I should just embrace my sorry, pathetic side and go on with my life, but I just can't. Why is that?"

K changed the subject. "Your patch looked bigger yesterday. People think you're letting it show deliberately. They're calling you a bitch, like the villains in your stories."

"Are you serious?"

I burst out laughing before she could answer. I laughed so hard tears streamed down my cheeks. Covering the mouthpiece with my hand, I laughed even more. Sensing this was going to last a while, I took a seat, still convulsing with laughter. This is hilarious. Did everyone know I was this funny?

The Other Side of the World

With her red pocketknife, she digs him out of his dead, meaningless reality. Dangling from the knife's tip, he watches as his past flashes before his eyes.

She gets up to smoke a cigarette. He's not in their bed. She discovers him in the living room, lying on her long wooden bench. This is how she always finds him. Whenever he sees narrow rectangles long enough to hold him, he has to try them out, muttering to himself as he does so. *This one's too narrow. I'd have to fold my bones to fit on it. This one's too long. I'd have to grow an inch. This one's too plush. Too much temptation.* He tries out different benches as if he's shopping for a coffin. He has yet to find the perfect rectangle.

The bench he's on now was custom-built by a carpenter, but he still complains. *My body's changing, shaped by time. This bench doesn't fit anymore*, he'd murmur, and he'd curl up on the floor where the sunlight from the living room window had created a white rectangle of light.

Lighting her cigarette, she approaches him. His eyes are open but unseeing. Nothing—not her sagging breasts poking through the dirty lingerie, not her wrinkled, sweet face, not her tough resourcefulness—makes an impression on him.

The door to the smaller room opens and the woman's young daughter appears. Her mother scolds her, *I heard you hit a classmate yesterday and lied to your teacher. When I came home last night, you weren't in your bed. Why can't you act like a normal child?* The girl doesn't respond. She slips across the room and peers down at the man, as her mother did moments before.

Annoyed, her mother rubs out her cigarette and storms off to her room.

"Mister?" the little girl asks. "Why do you only sleep with my mom? Why won't you sleep with me?"

Her voice isn't that of a child's. It sounds like it existed before the dawn of time. It has no tone, no color. It exists only to carry meaning in the words that float to where he is on the bench. "Men sleep with women, don't they? I'm a woman," she continues.

Still on his back, he answers, "You're too young."

"I don't understand," the girl responds. "Exactly how old should I be? When are you considered too young? Is there a height and weight requirement? How much taller and bigger do I have to be? Adults make rules all the time. Then they punish people who break them. Sometimes they make new rules. Do they have a rule to describe how young is too young? I know rules are convenient to have when you're living with a lot of people. I want to know what they are, so I can know to keep them."

"It's hard to put a number on how young is too young," he explains. "It's too abstract a concept. Instead, you can try to narrow it down. It's not that you're too young per se, but you're too young to sleep with a man."

The girl isn't satisfied. "Too young to sleep with a man, or too young to sleep with you? Your words are too hard. My dad explained it better. He said people who like each other sleep together. I like you, so I want to sleep with you, but you say I'm too young. I don't understand what 'too young' means so I'm asking you to explain, but all you're doing is saying the same thing, that I'm too young to sleep with you."

With that, she runs to her room and slams the door shut. He lifts himself from the bench. He washes his face, shaves, and gets his bag. The woman makes him coffee.

"How many days will you be gone?" she asks.

"About ten."

"Where are you going this time?"

"São Paulo."

There's a short silence. Her voice sounds ragged when she speaks again, "When you come back, I think we need to talk."

She stops stirring her coffee and gives him a pointed look. He's drinking from his cup, not looking at her. In fact, she can't remember if he answered her questions. It's as if he's not here. Sighing, she stays quiet for a long time. He might not have set foot in this house at all.

Maybe the bastard was never even born, she thinks to herself as she hurries to go to work.

He checks his plane ticket for the departure time. October 27, 18:40. Only then does he realize it's his birthday. The woman's wrong. He'd been born.

Settled in his seat on the plane, he looks out the window. The plane sprints down the runway, sweating from the exertion. Panting, it draws in one last breath before suddenly thrusting itself into the sky. That's when he gets the headache.

It feels like someone has detached his head from his body and bound it with strips of cloth with a knot at the top that digs into his scalp. Migraines have become part of his life—pain he can depend on. If not this, he'd have developed some other kind of pain.

He kneads his forehead with one hand, using the other to remove the in-flight magazine from the seat pocket. He turns the first page and sees a map of the world with numerous red dots and curves denoting travel destinations and routes. He looks for Brazil. There are pictures of São Paulo citizens gesturing inside telephone booths shaped like antique hair perming machines. Samba dancers toss their heads back in laughter, wearing elaborate dresses that don't seem to weigh them down. Bikini-clad girls are roasting on the beach. The Iguazu Falls is captured in a majestic spread.

He thinks back to the wall calendar in the woman's house with its predictable photos of sunrises for January and February, flowers for March and April, greenery for May and June, beaches for July and August, autumn leaves for September and October, then snow to round out the remaining months. Brazil doesn't have such distinct changes between the seasons. How did its first people determine New Year's Day? In countries with annual farming cycles, planting and harvesting delineate the seasons. In a place where sleeves are never worn and the same fruit can be found all four seasons, this becomes more of a challenge. When does one begin? How do we know when a year ends?

Or maybe he's complicating things. Maybe Brazilians had access to another country's calendar, which they used to align their lives. In essence, it's really calendars that complicate things, not the lack thereof. There's no need to mark one year's end and another's beginning. People merely need to live their lives, that's all.

He smiles to himself. It's no use. After all, people can't go through life without being governed by time. Time exists to separate yesterday from today. Save for the fact that yesterday was October 26 and today is October 27, nothing has changed. To him, numbers don't stand for size or order. All numbers do is distinguish one thing from another. Different number, nothing new.

Whenever a new season began, the woman delighted in digging last year's clothes from the closet. *You wore this jacket last spring, remember? I bought these jeans for you at Namdaemun Market.* The fact that he'd worn those clothes sometime in their past was her way of differentiating between then and now. Through the clothes, she reconfirmed the fact he was still with her. He smiled. Only by reminding himself of the person he spent last winter with could he sense the passing of time.

That, however, is not possible in Brazil. How do people make cherished memories there? He needn't worry though. He hates partitioning, and has no memories worth cherishing anyway.

He decides to drink some wine to dull the headache. He'll have to turn and press the button that calls for a flight attendant. His thoughts stop upon arriving at the need to locate the button. They don't prompt him into action. He remains motionless.

The old man next to him, whose teeth are heavily yellowed, asks if he's feeling pain. Wisely, he doesn't answer. But the old man is wiser. He can tell where the man's pain is coming from by the tell-tale palm pressed against the forehead. Beaming, the old man reaches down and brings out an old bag. He zips it open, peering inside with eyes as yellow as his teeth. His odor, together with his greasy clumps of hair, tells the man that this is a crafty individual. He probably has opium hidden in that bag.

The old man removes a small, flat tin case. He twists the lid open, re avealing a white powder. Using a spoon the size of a persimmon seed, he scoops some powder up. "Here, try this. It'll help you. Try it." When the man hesitates, the old man asks, "What, you think I'm a suspicious old man?" His black pupils, swimming in a sea of yellow, stare straight at his pursed lips. "This is bamboo salt. It can cure anything, I tell you."

He doesn't care if the powder is poison or medicine. Where was he? Ah, yes. Memories. He wants to ease his headache with the power of his thoughts. He wishes this old man would go away. He goes back to his thoughts, but as he has no memories to sustain them, they're no use. He regrets not having held on to a few memories.

The old man is too kind to leave him alone. He thrusts the small spoon up to his chin. His hand trembles feebly and some of the powder falls on the man's hand. He looks down at his hand and sighs, relieved, for he's just remembered something that will calm his thoughts. It's strong enough to suck him into its vortex, even if the memory isn't something he cherishes.

Riddled with financial troubles, his father had to close down the soda factory he ran for years. He announced he was leaving for Brazil. On the day of the memory, his father and uncle were discussing new ways to earn a living, debating what it'd be like to immigrate to another country. As a young man, his uncle was an industrial painter. When ships came to dock, he brushed a fresh coat of paint over their rusty hulls, and after the ships set sail, he took to drinking until they came back. When he got married, his brother—the man's father—gave him work at the soda factory. When it went under, they both lost their jobs.

It was a very cold day. The man, then a young boy, was inside the abandoned factory, sprawled out on a discarded pallet. Here and there, frozen glass soda bottles were cracking under pressure. Pop! One broke right in front of him. He reached over, picked up a shard of glass, and began playing with it. He peered at the frozen chunk of soda still inside the bottle. Once liquid, it was now solid. He played with the ice and glass, later mistaking one for the other. At first, he didn't notice the blood or feel the pain. His cousin, a girl one year older, dabbed ointment on his wound. He asked, "Why am I the only one in pain?"

"Because you're the only one who got hurt," she responded.

"Why didn't anyone else get hurt?"

"Because everyone else behaved."

"So if you behave, you don't get hurt?"

"Kids who behave don't get hurt."

"Are there other kids like me?"

"Somewhere, maybe." Suddenly, she shrieked. "You idiot! You made me get ointment all over my hand! And I'm missing dinner because of you!"

As a boy, he, like the girl who'd asked to sleep with him, wasn't satisfied with many of the answers he received.

"Where is she?" he asked his cousin stubbornly.

"Where's who?" she muttered distractedly.

"The other kid who doesn't behave."

"Who cares? Maybe she lives on the other side of the world."

She must be in pain, too. I can't be the only one. We're both suffering, he'd thought.

His cousin left for Brazil that year, but he couldn't go because his father, mother, and older brother were all dead. They were murdered by a former employee of his father who'd worked at the factory before he was born. A few days before the family was to flee to Brazil, the employee came to see his father, a kitchen knife tucked under his belt. Grabbing his father by the collar, he screamed for his late wages. And then, like a page out of the local newspaper, he lost it and stabbed all three members of the man's family in "a wild killing spree."

But he let the boy go. He found the boy with a spinning top in his hand, a top he'd made for the child. The boy stared at the bloody knife, just inches away from his nose. He couldn't tell if the dripping blood belonged to his father, mother, or brother. The top was painted red, yellow, and blue. When it spun, the three colors blended together in a crazy whirl. The killer had gotten the paint from the boy's uncle.

The uncle left for Brazil on his dead brother's money. The boy didn't go with him; he was sent to Hope Orphanage instead. His uncle wrote to him sometimes. He also sent money. Those letters and money saw the boy into adulthood.

Now, it's his cousin's letter, not his uncle's, in his bag. She'd written to tell him that her father, his uncle, was dying and that he wanted to see his nephew one last time. She assumed he wouldn't come, but couldn't deny her father his last wish. She sent him plane tickets with the letter. She wrote that she was going to mail it to his old address since she didn't know where he was staying.

It was the woman's young daughter who found the letter. *Mister, you have mail. Is this letter going to make you go away? Mom said you might leave one day. She said you'll leave when someone tells you to come to them. She said not to tell anybody you're here if I want you to stay with us. But I know you're here. Does that make me 'anybody'?*

He took the letter from her hands and closed the door to his room.

The plane is flying above the skies of L.A. He looks down at the sprawling city, at its tiny curving roads and the blue swaths he made out as swimming pools. An announcement came on. *Ladies and gentlemen, welcome to Los*

Angeles. The current time now is 18:45, and it's October 27.

He resets his watch. He left Seoul the night of his birthday, and now, he's greeted with another birthday. His time in flight—the headache, the battle of wits waged with the old man, the hours of sleep—have disappeared without a trace.

Setting back his watch, he accepts what happened. He had dinner before falling asleep a few hours ago, but the flight attendant is bringing him another. His plane flew eight hours back in time while he slept. It was suspended in air, but had traveled through time.

Slowly chewing his food, he lets his mind wander to the international date line. He began his trip on the other side of the line. Now he finds himself on the opposite side. That gives him twenty-four new hours. When he goes back, he'll lose the twenty-four hours. He's crossed the line into today. When he goes back, he'll be living in tomorrow. Back: tomorrow. Forth: today. He goes the other way. He pretends he's going back to yesterday. That means it's today where he is now. What was today is now yesterday, and what should be tomorrow is now today.

The passengers have to all get off in L.A. They follow an employee with a sign to a lounge where they wait for about an hour. After that, they get on another plane to fly twelve more hours. Brazil is far away. It's on the other side of the world.

He falls asleep immediately upon boarding the new plane. His headache has worsened. He never sleeps comfortably, with or without headaches. In fact, he can't remember the last time he had a good sleep.

Waking up, he groggily hears the captain announcing, *Ladies and gentlemen, welcome to São Paulo. The current time now is 07:10, and it's October 28.* The old passenger who sat next to him has to fly several more hours to get to Argentina, where his daughter lives. The old man doesn't look down to set his watch, probably waiting until he arrives in Buenos Aires. Or maybe he's not wearing a watch.

Adults make rules based on numbers so everyone can know what they mean, the young girl had said. According to these "rules," he'd flown for only one night, but in reality, he'd been on airplanes for a full twenty-three hours. He's exhausted.

After exchanging dollars into *cruzados* at the São Paulo airport, he climbs into a taxi with only two doors. He shows the driver the address his cousin gave him, and the driver sets off.

His uncle has already been dead for over ten days. Everyone thought he'd live, as the bullet had missed his vital organs, but he died after two weeks. His wife's shoulders shake as she wails that this isn't the way a man should go, killed by a robber in a foreign land.

"This robber only held up Korean stores," the man's cousin explains. "He didn't just steal money; he always left a dead body behind. He's a fucking nut job. Most Koreans in São Paulo own clothing stores. Many work at garment factories, too. They're all hard-working, so they make good money. The robber knew their habits, what time they took their meals, where they kept their money, what the insides of their stores looked like. That's why the police couldn't catch him. How did he know Koreans so well? Well, it turns out his boss's girlfriend was a Korean chick. She was arrested last week when she left a pocketknife in one of the stores. If we'd gotten to her first, we'd have ripped her into shreds. How could she do that to her own people?"

Race must matter a lot here, the man thinks. In Korea, it's harder to kill someone who's not of your race. In fact, murders occur more frequently within the much narrower scope of kin, as he himself could attest.

"Killing is so common here," his cousin continues. "Even the police can be hired to kill." Suddenly, she grabs his arm and offers to give him a tour of the city "Let's go see São Paulo. You'll need to find a place to stay, too."

The streets are dirty. He stops before an old gate leading up to nothing, no house, no walls. Beyond it lay three bank buildings, but they're not what the gate is for. Approaching it, he tries to decipher the words carved on the outside, but can only make out the date—1896. That makes the gate one hundred years old. It must have protected a house back then. Someone must have walked past the gate to get to his house. It now stands in a lot cleared to build more banks, but the gate itself hasn't been demolished—perhaps because of cherished memories.

He has no memories to hold on to, but he suddenly feels like something that's been kept inside of him has changed. He feels the burden of recollection.

It's strange, the way he senses that load. First, he feels something being unearthed from inside of him. Only then does he realize there was something there in the first place, and that it's been dragging him down with its weight. Once he's rid of the burden, he can appreciate how heavy it was. He ponders that for a moment. The only change he can think of is the knowledge that his uncle is dead.

"Well? Don't you think it's shocking what that woman did?" his cousin asks, her voice far away.

He gets a room in a small hotel in Little Asia. His cousin insists São Paulo is best experienced at night. She leaves after promising to pick him up at seven. He slams the door behind her, then he goes into the bathroom and turns on the tap. It refuses to flow. He realizes he has to turn the knob the other way. He's halfway around the world; faucets have to be turned the opposite way.

In the shower stall, he looks down at the water swirling into the drain. The hole sucks in the water, taking his filth with it. The water flows to the right. He's unsure whether this is clockwise or counter-clockwise. Brazilian clocks could go right to left; who knows? Or maybe its people have figured out how to tell time differently. His thoughts wander to his girlfriend's daughter again. *I know rules are necessary when you're living with other people.*

His cousin reappears at night wearing a crop top that shows off her midriff. She loops an arm into his. He struggles to loosen her grip.

"Let's go," she chirps.

"Go where?"

"Somewhere fun." Her earrings jingle every time she talks. He tells himself this bizarre behavior is her way of coping with her father's death.

The bar they go to—Bagong—is crowded with over twenty women, none of whom are decently clad. Some are dancing, others are drinking. Some women are dancing on stage, while others are rubbing their tits against drunk men. He sees a woman dancing discreetly behind a wall, but soon, she also lets her inhibition run free and wildly rushes the stage. Everywhere he looks there are dancing female bodies.

The music suddenly dies down, and a man and woman, both naked, appear on stage. They begin wrestling, incorporating strange techniques. The woman, for instance, seems to be doing a study on body contortions. Otherwise, she wouldn't be doing something that looked so painful. The man seems intent on learning about balance. That's the only explanation for why he's thrusting and writhing so intensely.

They wrestle together, and apart. Finally, they become entangled in each other's arms until suddenly, the woman screams and collapses. Her body slips away from him, revealing the man's naked crotch to the crowd. White juice dribbles down his leg. The fight is over, but there's no chance of rest for this couple, who hurriedly pick up their whips and leather straps and disappear behind the stage.

His cousin is dancing in her seat. The bouncing lights make it appear as if he's dancing as well, which he's not. What he is doing is seeing how long he can hold his breath against the overwhelming smell of perfume and sweat. He checks the seconds on his watch, his breath sucked in. When he can't stand it anymore, he quickly draws in a short breath and holds it. He times himself again. The seconds become shorter and shorter. He's drawing in breaths quicker and quicker.

His cousin drags a black girl to where he's sitting. He sees them coming as he's holding his breath.

"This is a friend of mine," his cousin introduces them and sits her next to him.

She—the black girl—says hello, then sits there smiling, as that's the extent of the conversation they can have. He isn't exactly nice to her, but he has no reason to be rude to her, either. He turns to face the girl. She grins again, showing off a set of dazzlingly white teeth. He can't smile back as he's in the middle of drawing in his breath.

His cousin gets up again and walks over to a fat blond girl in a pink bra. The girl shouts in broken English, "I can be occupied in eighty dollars. Can you pay ninety dollars?"

He draws in another big breath. The blond girl sees his wide, bulging eyes, raises an eyebrow, then leaves, bidding them good night.

Good night, he mutters to himself, done with this game.

He wakes up late the next morning. He remembers making another stop with his cousin after leaving Bagong.

"Where are we? This isn't my hotel," he'd protested.

"Go on in. It's a great place."

Never a fan of confrontation, he got out of the car. The black girl, who'd been hunched like a shadow in the back seat, climbed out with him.

They arrived at a door connected to the parking lot. It led to a room bathed in a shimmering blue. In the middle of the room was a big tub with lights in the floor. A soft cobalt glow washed over the entire room.

Facing the tub was a pool. The black woman slowly made her way to it, then, sweeping back the fronds of a palm tree, pressed a hidden button. The domed ceiling split open, revealing a night sky exploding with stars. The black woman shed her clothes and dove into the glimmering pool.

The room's four walls were covered entirely in mirrors. He took one step to the right and saw dozens of himself mirrored back to him. Suddenly, his knees snapped and clicked, as if a lock had been turned. He couldn't move.

The black woman emerged dripping from the pool and approached him. She got down on her knees and began licking his leg. He thought of what his cousin had said. "Brazilian women do as they're told. They don't think that's beneath them. What really hurts their pride is when they're paid less than what they thought they'd get."

He gave the woman money. He can't remember much else. His headache is back. It's the same aching pain of having his head tied and bound. He wonders if it's possible to choke someone by the head rather than the throat. Maybe the pain isn't caused by external pressure; maybe something inside his head is trying to claw its way out. A change of perspective is what he needs.

Since his uncle is already dead, he pushes his flight up from Friday to Tuesday. Soon, he finds himself sitting in São Paulo airport.

The breakfast of beef stew he had that morning at Anamoto, a Korean restaurant in Little Asia, isn't settling well in his stomach. The chef had told him he'd run away from a fishing boat and ended up in São Paulo. He was the restaurant's cook and only employee, so he alone was responsible for the terrible food. Before he left, the cook had asked him to deliver a yellow envelope to a friend of his. It was uncomfortably heavy. *It might be a gun,* he'd thought but quickly discarded the idea as childish.

He thinks about the old man he met on the plane who had opium in a tin can. Or was it bamboo salt? It had to be opium. It might have been salt. Did he reset his watch in Argentina? Did he even have a watch? Bored with these questions, he stops speculating and lies down on a row of chairs inside the terminal.

He sees an older white lady sitting in a chair across from him. Red pins hang from her wild, bushy hair. Even in this heat, she's wearing a khaki trench coat. She's knitting, but upon closer inspection, it appears the needles aren't looping into any yarn. She's knitting thin air. She's not wearing any shoes.

Suddenly, she gets up and sees him reclining on the chairs. She looks surprised. She approaches quietly and peers down at him. Grinning, she shouts hello. Shocked, he almost sits up. Once she's greeted him, she tucks her knitting under one arm and marches off to a phone booth. The red pins dance in her hair.

Removing a coin from her coat pocket, she sticks it in the slot, not the intended slot but where you're supposed to collect your change. She starts talking excitedly into the receiver, oblivious to the passage of time. Three people are waiting for her phone call to end. The man standing behind her taps his foot impatiently before leaning in and realizing that the woman is not, in fact, speaking at all. Her lips are moving, but no sound is emitted. Angrily, he grabs the receiver from her hand. She screams. He's furious, she's shrieking. She's gesturing wildly, waving her knitting bag in the air.

His cousin returns with a couple of drinks.

"Her?" She explains. "That woman's been doing that for years. She pretends to knit and talk on the phone, then she accuses people of trying to steal her purse. She's nuts."

Two airport employees drag the crazy lady away by her arms. She looks as happy as she did when she was on the phone. She's smiling, with her head leaning against one of the guards. Her bare feet are surprisingly clean.

The pins are still dangling from her hair, like fruit hanging from a tree whose roots must be near her eyes or ears. Those roots might hold her memories. She has so many of them that her mind lacks the space to contain them all. Only by removing herself from her memories can she realize how big a space they took up, the same realization he'd stumbled upon at the hundred-year-old gate.

As soon as he takes his seat on the plane, he turns to look out the window. The plane roars down the runway and takes off just before losing its breath. He changes planes in L.A. again. He goes to sleep when they turn off the overhead lights. He dreams the longest dream of his life.

In this dream, he's returned to São Paulo, where a strange woman is waiting for him. She seems overwhelming somehow. He considers her outfit to be the cause of this. Tight leggings wrap her legs. Colorful beaded sandals bind her feet. Even after figuring out what he thinks is the reason, he's still uncomfortable. He suspects there's more to this overwhelming feeling. He's annoyed that his heart's beating so quickly. He doesn't know how to control it.

He looks down and sees her hand, a scar etched into its skin.

"I got hurt on a boat that brought me to São Paulo when I was a girl," she tells him. "We sailed for what seemed like forever without any sign of land. I threw up greenish water and stumbled out to the deck. It was filled with rusty metal. When I got seasick, I played with a pocketknife, scraping it against the rust. I liked the sound it made, plus the smell of metal eased my nausea. One day, I was playing with my knife when I heard my brother approach. I slit my hand trying to hide the knife from him. My brother rubbed ointment into the broken skin. 'Why am I the only one in pain?' I asked.

"He said it was because I was the only one who was hurt. I asked him why no one else was hurt. He told me everyone else behaves. I asked him if kids who behave get hurt. He said no. I asked him if there was anyone else who was no good, like me. He told me to shut up, and accused me of stealing his pocketknife. I demanded to know where the other kid was.

'Where's the other kid who's no good?'

'How should I know? Maybe there are plenty of stealing bitches in poor countries. You should have stayed in Korea and lived as a thief, you stupid bitch.'"

He takes the woman to the São Paulo Cathedral. On their way, he stops to buy fruit from a stand. With his pocketknife, he digs into the red, pulpy flesh of a papaya, which they share. The cold, sharp blade becomes sticky with juice. They laugh as the slippery fruit disappears down their throats. The knife's point presses into their greedy, twisting tongues. They shiver with delight.

Inside the church, he says, "It's strange. I feel like I've been here before."

He looks at the curved road leading to the street market. "Really," he continues, "I remember running down that road and stealing roast sausages from a stand."

"Do you remember praying in front of the Jesus statue?" She asks. "We asked God to take your cousin and my brother. When God failed to answer, we stopped praying. Remember?"

Behind the cathedral, they spot a wooden bench. It has the most perfect rectangular shape they've ever seen. They quickly run over and lie on the damp, smelly bench.

Bugs crawl on them. They feel dozens of tiny feet wriggling over their skin. Worms writhe, their hairy heads still as their humps rise and fall.

They've seen these worms before and remember believing their feet would feel scratchy on human skin. They were wrong. The sensation is more itchy than rough. Covered in dirt and hair, the plump, greenish worms look as if they'd burst into a soggy mess if squeezed. When the bugs crawl over their lips, they bite into their flesh and slurp their insides.

There's no end to the worms. Lying on the perfect rectangle, they find themselves increasingly covered in soft, pulpy bugs. They look like they're lying in a shallow grave, the slow procession of hairy green worms like grass gently swaying in the breeze. They fall asleep beneath the blanket of worms. They've never had a more peaceful rest.

They discover another rectangle while frolicking in the waters of Santos Beach. They climb onto the rectangle and sail across the sea. As they run across the sand, the joints in their unused, rusty knees click into place.

Opening their mouths, they drizzle sour saliva over each other's tongues. At first, the caves of their mouths are cold and empty. Later, they feel their tongues soften and come to life. Now their tongues are hot as fire and hard as ice.

Using their hands, they reach deep into each other's mouths. They move past the ribs and grope each other's hearts. They feel their way down the esophagus and stroke the excrement piled up in the bowels. Slowly, they fold their own bodies into each other.

Once inside, they feel at home. They don't need to know where one body begins and the other ends. They feel complete. He speaks, "You're the one who killed my uncle."

Suddenly, they hear laughter. His father, mother, and brother are staring at them.

She looks into his eyes. "Your eyes are so pretty. I want them."

He removes one eyeball and hands it to her. Even in the palm of her hand, his eye looks adoringly at her. He thinks, "That's strange. I took out an eye but it doesn't hurt at all. This is a painless world. I must be dreaming."

He finally stops to consider that this could be a dream. He drifts back through memory. He remembers changing planes in L.A. to get to Korea. Then he fell asleep. *This must be a dream.*

His eyelids slowly open.

Ever since he came back from Brazil, she feels, he's been different. He still doesn't say much, but these days, when she hurls insults at him, a smile plays at his lips. She feels the change when she's holding him in her arms. She can feel a warmth. Before, sex with him was like fucking a stick, nothing more. It was as if he gave her his dick to use while the rest of his body turned away from her and slept. He was never present. But now, he leaves his warmth imprinted in the places he's been.

She wants to know what happened to him in São Paulo. He says he had to visit someone there. *Did things go well there?* a part of her wants to ask, but another, better part of her hates to dwell on problems.

One day, after she's left for work, he packs his things. Her daughter emerges from her room. She sees the two bags he's packing. He takes a pocketknife from the smaller of the bags. It's red with a silver cross on its side.

"Take this." He hands it to her.

"Are you leaving for good? Did someone ask you to leave? Is that it?"

"Yes," he answers.

"Does that mean I can't sleep with you?"

"Yes. Use this knife to remove all thoughts of me from your mind."

The girl begins to cry.

"I've never seen you cry before. You're cute when you cry."

"I've never had anyone call me cute before," she sobs. "Every day I was growing taller so I could one day sleep with you."

For the first time, he realizes how painful it is to say goodbye.

He grabs his bags. He turns toward the wall, where a map of the world is pinned. Two small holes have been poked into the map, indicating Brazil and South Korea. From a distance, they look like the black pupils of someone's piercing stare.

He removes the map and rolls it up, and the two countries meet as one.

Summer Is Fleeting

Oray was at the door. When he buzzed the doorbell, Hyuk-hee glanced in my direction.

"You go answer the door."

"No, you go," I muttered.

"You own this house," Hyuk-hee retorted.

We were sitting motionless with our backs to the wall. The heat was unbearable. Sweat coursed down our necks and behind our ears. The folds in our crotch were sticky to the touch. Our tired, limp dicks, shapeless as smeared horseshit, peeked from our boxers. Our faces were red and glistening with sweat. I probably had it worse, my enormous, flabby stomach about twice the size of Hyuk-hee's, but Hyuk-hee was heaving just as hard, his thick chest hair slicked down with sweat.

The buzzing became louder and more insistent. Hyuk-hee complained, "I'm too depressed to move. My girlfriend dumped me last night."

Ten months out of the year, Hyuk-hee was nursing a heartbreak. The buzzing was getting out of control.

"Open the door. Maybe he needs to take a whiz."

"Maybe if we wait long enough, he'll let himself in."

"Good idea."

The door swung open. It was always unlocked, but no good news ever came through it. In walked Oray, pointing his finger like a gun. *Bang!* He always announced himself like that.

"Did I get you?" Oray asked.

"Yeah, six times," I mumbled through closed lips, still leaning against the wall.

"Seven, including that mouth you're always running." Oray moved to pretend-shoot me again.

My weight had held steady at one hundred eighty-three pounds for ten years. After I was exempted from army service on account of being underweight, I took to wolfing down eight hamburgers and a liter of milk every night before bed. For those two years I should have been in the army, I made good use of my time. I gained weight every night.

Oray was covered in sweat. His light khaki shirt with the Superman logo on the front had turned a putrid green. He was holding a plastic bag stamped with the green 7-11 logo.

"You bought a Superman shirt?" Hyuk-hee asked, barely lifting his head the few inches he needed to look up at him.

"Yeah, and I got a free pair of tights to go with it," Oray replied as he removed items from the bag. Pulling out a beer, he asked, "Who asked for the maxi-pad with wings?"

"I did," I answered, not bothering to look up.

"Did you want overnights?"

"Yeah. I wear them to bed at night."

"Who wanted the KY jelly?"

"I did," I answered.

"And the Korean flag?"

"Me again."

"Get up."

Oray had lined up a yellow bottle of Miller Lite, a blue can of Cass beer, and a Heineken in its trademark green bottle on the table. The rest, he put in the fridge.

Laboriously, Hyuk-hee and I gripped the floor with one hand and used the other to help each other to our feet. A page from a tabloid newspaper clung to our legs. Hyuk-hee peeled it off with his foot. A dried up ramen noodle was stuck to his toe. I had a bit of ramen seasoning on one knee.

"And the movie? I told you to rent a Hong Kong film," I sniffed.

"*She's Going to Hong Kong* or *Take Me to Hong Kong*?" Oray asked.

"Yeah."

"The store was out of those. They only had martial arts films—*Man in the Hole, The Abandoned Hole, The Hole in the Wall.*"

"Did you rent them?"

"No. I couldn't find which hole they were in."

The three of us sat at the table and helped ourselves to the beer and pistachio nuts Oray had bought. Oray grabbed the Miller Lite, Hyuk-hee the Heineken, and I the Cass. The can was still cold. When I grabbed it, the chilled aluminum surface immediately became imprinted with my fingers. With one swig, I felt my body cool down. Oray got up and pressed the button on the CD player. Paul McCartney began singing. Oray dragged the fan out from behind our bed, plugged it in, and turned it on. That cooled the place down somewhat.

Of the three of us, Oray was the only one with an "activist conscience." He used to work as an aide to a politician, but after his boss lost the last elections, Oray was kicked to the curb along with nine unopened boxes of business cards. Now, he was sitting before us in a Superman t-shirt bringing justice to me and Hyuk-hee. His mouth ringed in beer foam, Hyuk-hee asked Oray, "What took you so long?"

"There was an accident."

"Were there fatalities?"

"237 deaths."

"Did you take a plane to 7-11?"

"Yeah. Everyone was ripped to shreds and their bodies tossed every which way. Workers are out there trying to glue the parts back together. There were at least eighty ambulances and fire trucks with tons of emergency workers," Oray continued.

"What were they doing?"

"Playing basketball with the decapitated heads. They aren't great dribblers though."

"At least they stitched you back together," I said. "Although they did a shitty job of it."

"I would have gotten here sooner if I wasn't stopped by a guy walking around with his head in his helmet."

"Did he accuse you of stealing his teeth? Did he demand them back?"

"No, but he glared at me with death in his eyes. He was terrifying."

"You're terrifying."

"It took the longest time to find my fingers. Apparently, I have twenty of them. And all this time I was only using four fingers to pick my nose. When I was little and begged my dad to buy me toys, he told me to play with my fingers instead."

Oray talked about his childhood often, but he was forgetful when it came to more recent events in his life. He argued that his forgetfulness was a survival instinct and said he wasn't going to apologize for it. He knew exactly what he wanted to forget, and forgetting wasn't easy. Right now, he was behaving as if he'd forgotten losing our game of rock-paper-scissors fifteen minutes ago, when that was the reason he'd gone out for the beer.

Oray reached for the 7-11 bag and rummaged in it. He retrieved several white envelopes. Hyuk-hee and I squinted at them.

"What are those?" Hyuk-hee asked.

"Mail."

Most of them were final notices to pay my gas, newspaper, and electricity bills. There was one from a credit card company announcing I no longer had access to their credit. One was addressed to a Mrs. Han, obviously delivered to me by mistake. The envelopes had been collecting dust for the past month in the mailbox of Apartment 304. Upon turning thirty-three years old this year, the three of us vowed to quit playing the card game *go*. But it appeared that Oray hadn't given up his habit of checking out what other players are holding.

"I saw what the woman in 303 has in her box."

At the mention of Apartment 303, Hyuk-hee and I swung our necks in Oray's direction. The woman in Apartment 303 has long hair. I'd only seen her twice. Once, she was wearing a baggy Lion King t-shirt over black leggings, her long, curly hair as wild and free as Julia Roberts' was in "Pretty Woman." She was on her way out and was locking the door to her apartment. It seemed to be jammed, as she had to push against the door with one foot while rotating the key in its lock. Red toenails poked out from her black sandals. Removing the key, she picked up a plastic basket from the ground and sailed off breezily, without even looking my way. She must have been headed to the spa on the basement floor of the 7-11.

I didn't recognize her the next time I saw her. She was in a chalk white business suit and stilettos with her hair in a stiff bun. She looked like a cross between a news anchorwoman and a cult leader. This time, she was trying to get inside her apartment, but the door was again giving her trouble. Using one foot to push against the door, she managed to get the key to turn. She disappeared inside without a glance in my direction.

Hyuk-hee said he ran into her every time he came to see me. Oray, who was usually over at my apartment when he wasn't participating in riots or working his shifts at the post office, pretended to know more about her than we did. We all referred to her as *The Woman*. Not even Oray could figure out her name from her mail. That was partly due to the fact *she* never got mail. Her utilities bills were addressed to "Ms. Kim Young-sook, Apartment 303." Kim Young-sook was our landlady. The power company listed her as the recipient on all bills delivered to apartment residents. I've been receiving notices for the past two months addressed to Kim Young-sook, Apartment 304.

"We can find out her name from her phone bill. The phone company asks for your name before registering a line." Oray showed off his worldly knowledge, probably gained from his many useless years in politics. Even he was at a loss, however, when we realized she didn't have a phone bill. We traded opinions on this mysterious woman.

"She might be hiding her identity. She's probably a secret agent trained in Sicily."

"Maybe she's illiterate and can't read."

"Or she might be mute. We know she doesn't own a phone."

"She might be an orphan that no one writes to."

"That's sad."

"I lost a sister in the Korean War."

"When I was President, I had women coming in every three months claiming to be my half-sister."

"We're all brothers of another mother."

"We're all deliveries."

After a couple rounds of this, we lost interest in the woman. The conversations always petered out after we'd offered our opinions on how best to manifest the destiny of our country.

So when Oray announced in a conspiratorial voice that he'd seen the woman's mail, we knew this time was different. Otherwise, he wouldn't have pulled metaphors from the game of *go*, the ultimate microcosm of human relationships and worldly wisdom.

"I saw what was in her mailbox."

Hyuk-hee and I, still not moving a muscle, stared at Oray's crooked teeth.

"There was a letter from Hankook Telecom," Oray continued. "Her internet bill. And it had her username."

"What is it?"

"LIAR." He announced triumphantly.

"Seriously?"

Hyuk-hee and I went back to drinking our beer. We looked on blankly as Oray made his way to the computer. In just a couple of clicks, he'd connected to the internet and searched her username in the database. Triumphantly, he read, "Name, Cho Heng. City, Seoul. Comments, none. Status, normal."

Hyuk-hee and I were quietly brushing up against one another, our fingernails idly scratching at the cans of beer.

"How've you been?" Hyuk-hee asked me.

"So-so. I've been working and studying, mostly," I answered.

"Read any good books lately?"

"Yeah. One. It was written by a woman and had a memorable cover."

"Was it a photo of her?"

"No, that was on the inside cover. There were blurbs of the publisher's newest releases."

"And?"

"Six of the eight releases were by other women authors. One woman published her book after years of hard work, one woman's book was a chilling record of the emptiness of life, one woman's prose was biting and relentless, and the rest contained lucid accounts of immense pain and terrible suffering. Is there anything more you want to know about women?"

"No," Hyuk-hee answered.

"What about men?"

"Men, I'm curious to know more about."

"Men whose dreamy prose fills an entire world? Men who write stories of society's underprivileged? Men who go on introspective journeys?"

"Men are awesome."

"Yeah."

"It's sad they stick out their necks so often."

"Sad."

Oray came back to the table. The three of us resumed drinking our beers. Later, Oray said, "I looked through all eighteen mailboxes but didn't find any acceptance letters."

"Yeah, this town has tons of mailboxes. It'll take you at least three years to dig through them all," I replied.

I used to work for IBM. Now I was waiting to hear back from other companies I'd submitted applications to. The only time my computer saw any love these days was when Oray came over.

The phone rang noisily. I looked at it without picking up.

"Aren't you going to answer that?" one of the guys asked.

"No," I replied.

Hyuk-hee, who was nearest to the phone, grumbled before picking up the receiver.

"Hello?"

Click.

Hyuk-hee put the receiver down. "I guess it was a wrong number."

We quietly drank our beers. Time was crawling at an excruciatingly slow pace.

"Is it hot or is it just me?" Hyuk-hee asked no one in particular.

"It's not you," I said.

"Want to tell stories to fight the heat?" Hyuk-hee suggested.

"Sure."

"Five guys left Busan to swim the Pacific Ocean."

"Who?"

"I don't know. Five young Korean guys."

"How do you know about this?"

"I copied a news article and named them the 'Mighty Five.'"

Hyuk-hee worked at a local newspaper staffed with the managing editor, one secretary, and one reporter. All he did was copy other news items. Even at karaoke bars, he'd be seen scribbling song lyrics into his notebook for future use.

"I have a story," Oray piped up. "It happened when I went back to my hometown after twenty years."

Not another childhood story. Hyuk-hee and I turned to each other and rolled our eyes like two symmetrical fractals.

Oray grew up in a mountain town notorious for its heavy snowfall. His parents worked on their farm all year, staying home only when the snowfall was so heavy that they couldn't set foot outside the house. Even then, his mother worked tirelessly, knitting sweaters for Oray, his older brother, and his younger sister. She used new yarn for his older brother and repurposed his old sweaters to give to Oray and his sister. When the long, dreary snow-

125

storm finally relented, Oray found himself with a new sweater made with old yarn. Now there was a ski lodge where once he and his sister had tumbled in the snow in their old/new sweaters.

"They built a ski resort where our town used to be. One day, I saw tanned kids from a neighboring village eating hot dogs and playing mini golf there. They said they'd come on vacation because farming season was over. How's that for a story to fight the heat?"

"It's pretty good."

Just then, the phone rang again. Hyuk-hee and I closed our eyes. Left without a choice, Oray reached for the phone.

"Hello?"

Click.

The first call could have been a prank. The second call could also have been a prank. Or maybe not. It could have been deliberate. The caller might have hung up because he'd expected to hear someone else's voice.

"The caller wasn't looking for me or Oray," Hyuk-hee thought out loud.

"Come to think of it, this apartment is yours," mused the always forgetful Oray.

"I'm not expecting any calls. Anyone who might call me knows the phone company cut me off," I yawned.

At that, Oray and Hyuk-hee lifted their eyebrows. I was surprised, too. If the phone company had indeed disconnected me, I shouldn't be getting calls in the first place.

"Maybe they still let you receive calls, but not make them."

"The new administration is all about reform, after all."

"Elections are drawing near."

The phone rang again. As the other guys watched, I lifted the receiver and pressed it to my ear. "Hello?"

It was no use. The caller hung up.

"I bet it's the girl who dumped me yesterday. My pager's broken so she's calling this number," Hyuk-hee guessed.

"She hung up when you answered the phone, too," Oray pointed out. Turning to me, he said, "Maybe that was a call about your job interview."

"It has to be a prank call. It's hot out," I concluded.

The three of us shared nothing in common. Hyuk-hee loved fiercely; Oray had never been on a date. He firmly believed the line in the French film *Happiness*: "Love is only hard in the beginning; once the connection is made, love becomes easy and repetitive." Hyuk-hee was always nursing a broken heart; Oray never had a girlfriend. As for me, there was nothing particular to say.

The phone rang again less than five minutes later. I unplugged the cord. The weather was intensely hot. We needed something more than an electric fan and cold beer.

Not long later, there came a knock at the door. It wasn't someone from the gas company or the landlady coming to demand I pay the utility bill. They'd have buzzed the doorbell. But this was a delicate, slightly annoyed knock. It had to be a woman. If she pushed the door, she'd realize it wasn't locked, but she was purposefully choosing to knock instead. One of us had to get up, but we did our best to look bored. The knocking continued, small and incessant, the way Aesop's grasshopper must have knocked at the ant's door. Finally, Oray, ever the acting conscience, got up.

From our table, we couldn't see the door very well. The back of Oray's shirt also bore the Superman logo. It was damp with sweat, but Oray was scratching his back, so we could only make out half of it. We briefly lost sight of him. Then he turned around and whispered, "Cho Heng."

Feigning boredom, Hyuk-hee and I lifted our beers to our lips at the same time.

"He says it's Heng at the door," Hyuk-hee muttered.

"So I heard."

"They're talking a long time."

"Maybe they're from the same town."

"Oray lives in Gangnam. We're in Seodaemun."

"Maybe she has another house in Gangnam."

Just then, we heard Oray's polite voice. "Would you like to come inside?"

The woman didn't come inside. When she left, Oray returned and gave us her message.

"She says she has AC in her apartment and invited us to come over."

"What else does she have?" I asked.

"Vigor panties?" Hyuk-hee suggested.

"Maybe her AC broke and she wants us to fix it," I guessed.

"Or she dropped a ring in the toilet," Hyuk-hee said.

"Maybe her boyfriend's zipper got caught in his bush."

"We'll need tools to get him out."

"Do you have your gun?"

Even as we were running our mouths, Hyuk-hee and I were looking for our shorts.

"She says she has coffee," Oray informed us.

"Is it old? Does she need us to finish it?"

"Does she want to fuck three guys at once then puke up all the coffee?"

"She already had two cups and she's fine," Oray said.

"Did she look okay?"

"More than okay."

Until that moment, we didn't know what we were getting ourselves into. The sun was almost setting, but the heat refused to let up. The wind stood absolutely still; there were no clouds in the sky. There was something perilous in the air.

A chill pervaded her house, and it wasn't from the AC. If it were, the air would merely feel cool. But this wasn't a sensation of coolness; it was most definitely a chill, like the forboding kind one might feel in a deserted temple at midnight or in front of a motel at the end of a long, narrow road. The scent of incense added to the feeling.

"Why did you light incense?" Oray asked.

"Because it hides the smell of cigarette smoke," she answered, as she lifted a cigarette to her lips. "They use this trick in Buddhist temples when they're barbequing pork."

The three of us nodded, then followed her uncertainly into the room. "The Lion Sleeps Tonight" was playing over the speakers. The lion sleeps tonight?

Her apartment was furnished with an old-fashioned couch and a coffee table hewn from dark wisteria wood. I sat on the floor, not wanting to topple over. My eyes wandered to several hooks on the wall, from which hung six panties with SUN, MON, TUE, and so on stamped on them. FRI was noticeably missing. I searched for a calendar, and found one conveniently hanging over the hooks. As I suspected, it was Friday. I went back to the panties and saw they were red, white, green, blue, black, and pink. She had to be wearing yellow.

She brought a tray with three oranges, one apple, a small knife, plates, and forks. There were also cookies which she'd probably bought at the neighborhood bakery that had opened a few days ago. She also offered us the old coffee. She was wearing a pink slip dress like the one Valerie Kaprisky wore in *Breathless*. Her eyes held the sly playfulness of a young girl who was scheduled to return to college after the summer but for now was willing to give in to reckless abandon and fall into the arms of a handsome Richard Gere.

Oray was perched on a round barstool. Hyuk-hee was the only one on the couch, so he was the one the woman sat next to. When she placed the tray on the coffee table, her breasts showed from beneath the deep V of her dress. They were small and unencumbered by a bra.

It was hard to determine her age. Her long hair was tied in a bun that revealed her mature, sophisticated neck, while her red painted toenails imparted a cheekiness. She must be in her thirties, as were we, but I decided she couldn't be older than thirty-three.

"We know a little about you," Oray began.

"Me?" Her eyes were lowered, trained on the orange she was halving. "What do you know?"

"We know your name, why you invited us, and how interested you are in us."

She burst out laughing.

"We know you're lazy, too," I added.

"How's that?" She stopped peeling the orange and looked straight at me.

"Because you leave your laundry hanging instead of tucking it away."

"Ah," she glanced at the panties and nodded twice, as if I'd gotten it right. I wanted to tell her I knew what color panties she was wearing, but stopped myself.

"There aren't any bras in your laundry though. Don't you wash them?"

"I don't wear bras." Then she pressed one of her nipples with a finger. It bounced back and traced a thin outline against her pink dress.

"How do you know my name?" she asked.

"The same way you found out my name and account number so you could pay my phone bill," I replied. Her eyes lit up.

"You knew about that?"

"That's why you called my place earlier, to see if the line was working and to see if we were home."

"I don't know," she frowned. "Did I have to check? There's always someone at your place."

"You wanted to find out if all three of us were there. We knew what you were up to. That's why we took turns answering the phone."

She burst out laughing again, and didn't stop for a long time. In the meantime, we nibbled on her cookies.

"Don't you just want to stay up all night talking to someone sometimes?" she asked, as she placed the orange sections on a dish.

"Never," all three of us shook our heads.

"We sleep at night."

"Or we watch TV until the programming ends and they play the national anthem. It's hard to sing along to the national anthem though. It'd be nice if there were lyrics that changed color to show you what to sing, like they do in karaoke."

The woman ignored us and continued, "I feel like talking sometimes, but not to someone I'm close to, and certainly not to a complete stranger. When I stumbled on your late payment bill in the mailbox, I thought that if I saved your phone line, I'd be the only one with access to the number."

"Oh."

"Do you know how it feels to have complete ownership of something?"

"No."

We were thirsty from the cookies, so we drank the coffee.

"If you paid for the phone, why didn't you call us?" Hyuk-hee asked, lowering his mug.

"We'd have been happy to hear from you," Oray added politely.

"I didn't have to call. Owning something means I can enjoy it whenever I want. It was enough to know I had you."

"Liar. You couldn't have called us even if you wanted to. You don't have a phone." Hyuk-hee still wanted to believe it was his ex-girlfriend who'd called us.

"I have a cellphone," she said, and pointed at her vanity. On it was a black Chanel bag, and next to that a cellphone and a crystal keychain holding three keys.

"We didn't see any cellphone bills in your mailbox."

"I have another address that I use for bills."

"What about this address?"

"I use this one to receive money."

"Do you get paid just for staying here?"

"Yes."

"How?"

"I have a man who pays me when I'm not with him."

"Liar," we retorted. After working through the oranges, she began peeling the apple.

"What are your hobbies?" Hyuk-hee asked her.

"Cooking."

"Liar. Your gas bill was only $1.60 this month."

She didn't respond.

Oray tried again. "What time did you go to bed last night?"

"I don't know. A little after twelve?"

"Liar. You were on the internet until 1:46."

After peeling the apple, she lifted her head and looked at us. "You figured out my username? What is it?"

"LIAR!" The three of us answered at once. She nodded. Then, cocking her head to one side and staring straight at us, she spoke slowly, "Now it's my turn to guess some things about you."

"Well, allow me to introduce ourselves," Oray said. He stopped and took a drink of coffee to wash down the cookie in his mouth.

"We're strong, able-bodied thirty-year-old Korean guys whom no one wants—except our country when it needed us to serve in the military," he continued. "We met ten years ago, on June 29, I think it was, at a coffee shop near City Hall that promised free coffee that day. Ever climbed to the top of Namhan Fortress? From there, you can see the whole of Seoul, a beautiful forest of skyscrapers and apartment complexes soaring majestically through the gray, smoggy sky. The sight's enough to bring tears to your eyes. Now imagine yourself standing awestruck before this magnificent scene when, suddenly, two men in a hang glider slowly drop down to where you're standing. When you turn to look, you see they're guys who are just like you. That's the kind of friendship we have.

"Now, a little more about us. One of us refused to go into the army. Since then, he's never obeyed any orders. That's why he's kicked out of every place he goes. One of us was busy sucking up to wealthy Gangnam ladies and borrowing money from his stockbroker friends for his boss, until he was dumped by those same ladies and his boss for not drumming up enough votes. He still has mountains of business cards with the word 'aide' stamped on them.

"I don't need to speak cryptically about this last guy. His name's Hwang Hyuk-hee. He's perpetually heartbroken, which means the only occupation he can decently hold is that of a poet."

"I think I know who's who," she said right away, her eyes sparkling. She turned to me first. "You're the one who didn't go into the army."

Turning to Hyuk-hee, she said, "You're Hwang Hyuk-hee."

To Oray, she declared, "Next year, you'll go back to those ladies and get their votes. That is, if you can manage to get through tonight."

"What are you, a mind reader?"

She laughed. "That's right. You got me."

"Are you serious, LIAR?"

"If you were paying customers, I'd feed you all the lies you'd want to hear, but I don't have to do that with you."

"No, you don't."

We fell silent. The smell of incense, briefly forgotten, wafted back to us and into our noses.

The CD player was on repeat.

"Do you like that song?" Hyuk-hee asked when "Lion Sleeps Tonight" started again.

"I liked it ten years ago."

"I see."

"Let's talk about songs we liked ten years ago," Oray suggested.

"The only song you know is 'Yesterday,'" Hyuk-hee argued.

"That's true."

"Why do you like that song so much anyway?"

"McCartney has to be the only twenty-year-old in the world who can sing about yesterday in such a flat, indifferent way." Hyuk-hee offered Oray an almond cookie. He stuffed it in his mouth. "When you're twenty, you don't think of time as something that's passing."

"I liked Sade ten years ago," Hyuk-hee offered. This time, Oray pressed a chocolate cookie in his hand, as if handing over the microphone. Hyuk-hee put it in his mouth. "Then I liked Vangelis. From there, I moved on to Queen, George Michael, and Boy George. The women I dated all gave me CDs as gifts. Why do all women act alike?"

"They can't help it. Look at Emma Bovary. I mean, why the hell would you give anyone a necklace with your photograph in it?"

"Women think that if they fall in love, that feeling's going to last. They don't realize that things change and disappear. They don't know what a pain it is to throw away old love letters and photographs. And yet, they're always the first ones to say goodbye. It's strange."

Hyuk-hee turned to the woman and asked, "One woman wrote me three different goodbye letters. You're a mind reader. Can you guess why she did that?"

"I need more details," the woman said as she also reached for a cookie.

"Then let's stop talking about old songs and move on to strange stories," Oray announced, like a debate moderator.

"In the first letter, she said she couldn't be with me, but that she still loved me. In the second, she announced she was leaving me *because* she loved me," Hyuk-hee explained.

"And the third?"

"She said she slept with another guy, and she loved him."

"That's the only letter where she meant what she wrote." The woman's eyes turned glassy and unseeing, like those of a possessed shaman. "When she wrote the first letter, she was seeing someone else who was probably living somewhere far away. He might have been relocated by his company or he might have gone to Europe to study. She didn't want to let go of him, but she also didn't want to lose you."

"By the time she wrote the second letter, her feelings for you had developed. She wanted to test her own feelings, and the letter was her way of doing so. She wanted to know if she'd be okay if she lost you."

"In the third letter, she's finally ready to let you go. If she confessed that she'd slept with another man, she obviously didn't care what you thought of her. One thing's certain." The woman tipped her head. "She never really loved you."

"I see," Hyuk-hee nodded, before adding, "I never got that third letter."

When the woman frowned, Oray quickly jumped in to clear the air. "We're supposed to be discussing strange stories."

The woman lifted another cigarette from her case. "Do any of you smoke?"

"We quit."

"On the same day."

"To commemorate quitting *go*."

She shook her head as we each offered an answer. The lit match in her hand shook with her.

"Your turn," Oray's gaze fell on me. I nodded, and hesitated. I always needed some time to rev up; I could never hit the ground running.

"Ten years ago, I went on a trip to the East Sea with two women—one with double eyelids, and one with no crease in her eyelids. I wanted to go with the second girl, but the double-lidded girl wanted to come with me. She was the one who suggested the trip. When I hesitated, she said the other girl would be joining us.

"When we arrived, we rubbed suntan oil on each other's backs and drank Coke underneath our big umbrella. We even had a race on the sand. The double-lidded girl laughed loudly, not caring what people thought. At night, we stayed in the same room, and because of the double-lidded girl's insistence, the other girl slept beside me, and she slept beside her. The other girl and I fell asleep right away, but the double-lidded girl stayed up all night, sobbing into her pillow.

"In the morning, her eyes were so swollen it made it painfully obvious that she'd had surgery done on her eyes.

"A few months later, she sent me a letter and a wedding invitation. She said that she was marrying someone who could never hurt her because she didn't love him."

"I knew this story was going to be boring." Oray and Hyuk-hee shrugged. I ignored them and continued, "Not long ago, I found out how she's doing."

"And?"

"She's doing very well. She gained weight, like I did."

"Is that the strange part?" Hyuk-hee asked.

"No."

"So what's strange about this story?"

"The strange thing is I can't stop thinking about her."

"No."

"Sometimes, I dream about her. In my dream, we're running on sand, but I'm so out of breath I can't catch up to her. First, the army didn't want me, and now I can't even run in my own dreams. I'm struggling to catch up when she turns around and flashes a smile. Her hair is blowing in the wind, and a saltiness chokes the air. Why do you think I'm having this dream?"

"You were twenty years old at the time," the woman replied coolly.

"So?"

"You're remembering your life as it was when you were twenty years old, the same way we hold memorial services to remember our ancestors," she analyzed.

"You're good at analysis."

"You should write a book. Freud did." Oray and Hyuk-hee were impressed.

I returned to my story. "After the trip, we came back to Seoul. It was the day of the general elections, so she and I went to the election booths and voted for the ruling party."

"Didn't you say this was ten years ago? The general elections were held in the winter, not summer."

"Were you even eligible to vote that year?"

"Okay, now this story's officially strange."

"Good job."

Oray and Hyuk-hee patted me on the shoulder. The mind reader, who'd been listening eagerly, looked cheated.

"You guys are just awful," she shook her head.

"And you're not a real mind reader."

"Why do you say that?"

"You already knew who we were."

"We've played this sort of game before."

"You only had to choose one answer out of three. Easiest multiple choice question there is."

She laughed.

We were getting bored, but we knew we'd still be bored if we left her apartment. It was better to stay where there was AC. Still, boring was boring.

"Do you have any beer?"

"I have some iced tea in the fridge. I don't drink alcohol," she replied, taking out another cigarette.

"Oray can go pick up some beer."

"We tell him what to get, but he always buys something else."

"Yeah. Earlier, I asked him to pick up KY Jelly but he got me a Heineken."

"KY Jelly?"

"Lube. Supposed to restore your sex life."

135

Lighting her cigarette, the woman turned to Oray. "Oray? Is that your name?"

"Yes."

"And your last name?"

"Pi!" Hyuk-hee and I answered for him.

"Pi Oray?"

"O, meaning 'the fifth' in Korean, and ray meaning 'to come.'"

"Were you the fifth child?"

"Third. I was born the year Ilray died."

"Let me guess. Is Eray the other brother?"

"No. Uray."

"Okay…"

"Aray died when he was five."

The woman shook her head, cigarette dangling from her lips. Ash fluttered onto my lap.

"Why don't we play a game?" Oray suggested.

"Game?" The woman asked.

"The three of us will each grant you a wish if you can answer one question."

"Wish?" Her ears perked up.

"One each, so three wishes in total. So, do you agree?"

The woman stubbed out the cigarette in a green glass ashtray. Remembering a story, Hyuk-hee spoke up.

"A long, long time ago, there lived three princes who were always fooling around and wasting time. One day, the oldest prince looked through his telescope and spotted a beautiful princess. She was, unfortunately, dying. The three princes decided they were bored enough to get on the middle prince's magic carpet and fly to her kingdom. They didn't have magic potions. They knew no tricks. They weren't great kissers, either. The youngest prince, however, had stolen an apple on the way to the kingdom (he was always stealing shit like that) and this saved the princess. Opening her eyes, she began to cry. She said that she hadn't eaten a thing in three days. She announced that she'd give herself to the prince who saved her life. Her one shortcoming was that she ate seven meals a day, but her immense beauty more than made up for that."

"Am I the princess?" the woman asked.

"If you can answer this question: Was it the telescope, the magic carpet,

136

or the apple that saved her."

"O.K., but I'd like to know what you're offering first," she replied.

"Then you'll give yourself over to us?"

"For one night, at least."

We broke into cold sweats under our t-shirts. Oray stopped scratching his back; Hyuk-hee brought a hand to his chest hair, as he always did when he was nervous. I was the only one who remained calm. I was better at hiding my feelings. Or maybe I was slower.

"So what do you want to do now?"

The woman took turns eyeing the three of us, then declared, "Let's go do karaoke."

According to Hyuk-hee, for something to be universally popular, it has to pander to the lowest common denominator. Entertainment for the few is found at the top; pleasure for the masses has to be gathered from below. To go wide, one must go down, Hyuk-hee believed. He's probably happier now stealing song lyrics than when he was a poet and had to pretend he knew all the secrets of life. He rationalized that copying song lyrics was his way of meeting the masses.

"Let's go do karaoke. The first person to find 'Love You More,' 'Love You,' and 'Love Because' gets to sing."

"Why those songs?"

"'Love You More' is sandwiched between the other two songs, so you can't search for it alphabetically."

"Let's do something else. Karaoke's not all that interesting."

The woman interrupted. "Can I tell you my wishes now?"

"Of course."

"I have two."

"Two?"

"One is to get out of this apartment."

We heaved a sigh of relief.

"That's not hard at all," Oray said.

"Leaving's easy; coming back isn't," she warned.

"Why's that?"

"I told you. You might not make it through the night."

"Oh?" Oray seemed nonplussed.

"It's not just you. Maybe none of us will."

"Really?"

"Either all four die, or just one does."

"Did you get that from *History of the Three Kingdoms?* In that book, there's a letter that if opened kills four people. If it stays unopened, only one person dies."

Ignoring Hyuk-hee, the woman kept her gaze on me and Oray. She asked, "Do you still want to go?"

We murmured among ourselves.

"If we don't survive tonight, maybe we'll make it through tomorrow night."

"Can we just get through tonight for now?"

"Let's talk about this outside?"

"Fine." The woman began clearing the plates and forks from the coffee table. "Where are we going?"

"We can go to the park and have some beers, maybe catch a drive-in movie."

"What about the amusement park? They're open at night. We can ride the roller coaster, then watch the parade and the laser show."

"And?"

"And have some beers."

"Fine."

"You said you don't drink."

"Tonight's special," she replied.

"Do the buses leave from Gangbyun Station or Gangnam Station? I think I saw an ad in the paper earlier."

"From both.

"What time?"

"I don't know."

"Go and find out, Oray. Go to Gangbyun first, and on your way back, you can stop by Gangnam Station. Or is it better to go to Gangnam first?"

"Maybe you'll be the one to get through the night."

"Don't get into a fight with a wrestler."

"Avoid lions, too."

Putting away the ashtray, the woman said, "I have a car we can use."

"What kind of car? We only ride Boeing 747s."

"A Volkswagen."

"Did you marry an old dude then poison his coffee? Are you one of those rich widows who use their husband's money to go clubbing at the

138

Hilton?"

"You got me again, Hyuk-hee," she said, and stood up.

"I'll drive. I'll grant your wish to leave the apartment," Oray said.

"I'll grant your wish to come back," Hyuk-hee offered. "That is, if we're still alive."

Standing up, I realized that she had only asked for two wishes, leaving me with no wish to grant. I was late, again.

We returned to my place to get ready. The apartment was as stuffy as a dim sum kitchen.

"It's hot in here."

"Yeah."

"I'm not sleeping here tonight," Hyuk-hee said confidently. "I'm sleeping somewhere with air-conditioning."

"Me, too," Oray and I responded.

Oray, who hadn't had a haircut in a while, pulled on a Chicago Bulls cap. Hyuk-hee spread gel in his hair and managed to find a shirt that wasn't completely filthy. They kept their shorts on. I changed into jeans. While pulling them on, I stepped on the nail clipper, which, unfortunately, had its blade pointing up like the wings of a cicada. Yelping, I hopped around on one foot. Oray glanced at me.

"Since you found the clipper, why don't you clip your toenails before we leave?"

He turned and saw Hyuk-hee putting his beeper in his pocket. "Why are you taking your pager when it's broken?"

"Real men carry guns, even if they've got no bullets," Hyuk-hee answered. "At least I can use it to check the time."

For the first time in a while, there was activity in the apartment. It was past seven in the evening but it was still light out.

The woman was waiting for us in the parking lot. She'd changed into a white cotton skirt and a jaunty pair of sneakers. The yellow polo shirt covering her flat breasts had the trademark Burberry checkered pattern on its collar. The shirt reminded me of her yellow panties.

She got behind the wheel, and Oray climbed into the passenger seat. Hyuk-hee and I sat in back. Every time I shifted in my seat, the car moved. Except for times like this, I forgot how heavy I was. The engine hummed to life.

"I thought I was going to drive," Oray complained, having lost the chance to grant her wish. He did have a forgetful streak, but he hadn't forgotten his desire to sleep in an air-conditioned room. It wasn't every day he got to sleep in a sexy mind reader's apartment.

"I don't trust other people's driving," she replied casually as she brushed her arm against his. "Let's say you did and leave it at that."

"But I didn't."

"But you can say you did. It won't matter. The car's moving, isn't it?"

"Why don't we just say you drove, too, and see if the car's still moving then?"

"Sorry. Are you going to get over this?"

"I'll try."

The Volkswagen began coasting downhill. This was the first time in two days Hyuk-hee and I had left the house. Our backs turned to each other, we stared out our respective windows. Some of the passing billboards were still lit. We arrived at the bottom of the hill. Hyuk-hee, his eyes still trained outside the window, asked, "What are we eating? Are we going to roast a zebra at the zoo?"

"The traffic in the city will get worse, so let's go someplace else. We'll eat when we come to a rest stop."

The woman clearly wasn't interested in eating. She glanced at her watch then turned the radio to the traffic channel, where an announcement was being made about a fatal accident on the freeway.

"The driver must have been speeding," the woman mused. "Better take the state road."

"Nothing goes right in my life," the woman began around the time we passed Hannam Bridge. "Nothing ever went the way I expected it to."

"You shouldn't have expected anything," Oray answered kindly. Hyuk-hee and I were debating whether to take a nap.

"My older sister and I had to go to work at a young age."

"Was her name Heng, too?"

"Soryu, meaning 'to bend' and 'to be fair.'"

"And your name means 'to go' and 'to be fair'?"

"'To be fortunate' and 'to be fair.'"

"Fortunate?"

140

"Or 'lucky.'"

"Lucky?"

"I used to work at a big rib joint. Now it's a chain restaurant with an American name."

"That was good thinking."

"My getting a job there?"

"No, your boss, modernizing the joint."

"You mean my ex-husband," she said as she turned onto the state road."

"Can you see the road in the dark?" Oray asked.

"Not really. But I know when I've crossed the double yellow line."

"Did you check the map before we left?"

"I tend to guess my way using the road signs."

"Guesswork is all you ever do."

She laughed abruptly. Then Oray asked, "Why are you driving so close to the car in front of us?"

"To intimidate him. He's so frustratingly slow."

"Have you considered you might be suffering from road rage?"

"It's a fact I'm proud of." Accelerating, she suddenly switched lanes. "I knew a guy who constantly gave orders from the passenger seat," she said. "He told me which lane to drive in. *Get in the first lane at the next intersection. After this stoplight, get ready to make a right.* He relayed all the stoplights and road signs, too. *Slow down, it's a yellow. Stop. Hold on. I don't see any traffic. You can run this one. Go.* I found myself driving blindly, just doing as I was told. Sometimes, we ended up lost, or were ticketed by a cop hiding in the bushes. I got furious at him when that happened, but when I did, his eyes would grow wide and he'd say, *But you're the one who's driving.* I felt cheated. But that made me stronger."

Oray nodded. "Did he have a license?"

"You mean a back-seat-driver's license?"

"Why do you only steer with your left hand?"

She stepped harder on the gas pedal. "Habit. Using only one hand, I can change signals, switch lanes, and flip the bird to other drivers."

"How'd you get that habit?"

"Guess."

"You're the mind reader."

"It's more fun to tempt fate instead of just playing it safe."

"Your passengers might not agree."

141

"Those aren't my words. They were the words of the guy who nagged me." She tapped the armrest with her right hand. "My real reason is that I needed my right hand to hold his hand. Once, I was doing 87 on the freeway and the guy fell asleep with my hand still in his. It was dark and raining, and my hand was sweating from the stress of driving in that. But I didn't want to pull my hand away and wake him."

"Strange."

"What is?"

"That he'd fall asleep with you next to him."

"Don't mock him."

"Do you like him?"

"He pays me."

Suddenly, a sharp piercing noise filled the air. Her cellphone was ringing in her purse, which was perched on Oray's lap. As he moved to get it, the woman spat, "Leave it."

She opened the console and fished around for a cigarette. She pressed the cigarette lighter. Her hand was shaking faintly. The ringing finally stopped, but after a few seconds, it began again. Smoke curled up from her cigarette. Hyuk-hee coughed a few times. It was his way of saying he wanted a drag, too.

"That was a customer," she said, to no one in particular.

"Do you moonlight as a call girl?"

"Do you read the horoscopes in the newspaper?" she asked.

"Exclusively. As for the rest, I only skim the pictures," Oray said triumphantly.

"I have a customer who calls hourly asking about his future. He was probably calling to ask if it's better to walk out of his house left foot first or right."

"Does he pay you a lot of money?"

"Enough. Why?"

"I think I can do what you do. It only involves choosing between two things."

"It's not difficult, that's true," she agreed. "But first you have to place everything in two columns, and that's not easy."

She threw out the half-smoked cigarette and lit a new one. Her hand was shaking. As she reached to put the lighter back in its jack, her left hand lost its grip on the wheel. The car jerked sharply to the left, but she quickly regained control. My eyes met Hyuk-hee's.

I think we're going to die tonight, my eyes said.

Yeah, Hyuk-hee seemed to say. *I guess we are.*

"I don't feel like dying, so could you drive with both hands?" Oray implored. The woman ignored him and used her left hand to lower the window and toss her cigarette out. *Apparently, she doesn't listen to men who don't pay her. Maybe she doesn't listen to any man. Maybe she was lying about everything.* I turned to Hyuk-hee. Our eyes met again.

She really is a LIAR.

Humid air rushed in through the open windows. The woman's long hair blew across her eyes. I saw her take her left hand from the steering wheel to roll up her window. When she did, the car went into a spin. In the next instant came a sharp, ripping noise, like a tire being torn to shreds. Our bodies lurched forward. Sparks flew. The car screeched to a halt. At least, I felt it did. I wasn't sure. It happened in the blink of an eye, and when it ended, a shocked silence fell. It lasted but moments.

"Blink your eyes at me," Oray commanded from the passenger seat. Hyuk-hee and I did as we were told.

"We're fine."

The woman had already left the car. No one was hurt. We all got out as well.

She'd hit a motorcycle, which had skidded all the way to the sidewalk. Its driver was a short, stocky man in a purple vest with Messenger Service emblazoned across the front. He wasn't on the ground. Instead, he was on his feet with his helmet tucked underneath one arm like a kamikaze pilot ready for takeoff. His eyes looked boldly at us.

"I'm fine. I'm not hurt," he smiled. "I know taekwondo and judo. When the accident took the bike from underneath me, I flew from the seat and landed on my feet."

Proud of this, he assured us again that he felt no pain. The woman argued that he needed to see a doctor, but he waved her off. On his thick, muscular forearm were tattooed the words *The Best or Nothing.*

"I told you, I'm fine. Just go."

We all gazed at him, clearly a good, brave guy. We were still gazing when he limped his way back to the bike. The woman ran after him. Trusting her to take care of the situation, we huddled under a sparsely leafed tree. It was getting dark. Hyuk-hee sat down on the sidewalk. I leaned against the tree, which moved slightly beneath my weight. The man and woman were still arguing. He was trying to leave and she was pulling his arm. Her yellow shirt and his purple vest were fading in the evening light.

"What a strange guy."

"What a strange woman."

"Who cares? We're in no hurry."

The man, good guy though he was, was finally nearing the end of his patience after twenty minutes of wrangling with this woman.

"I told you I don't need your money! If you're so rich, go help the poor," he said crossly.

"At least give me your address."

"Don't worry. I won't hunt you down."

"I need to know where you live."

"Why? So you can offer your condolences if I die?"

"Yes."

"Me? Die? Over this?" The man guffawed. "People don't die that easy."

At that, Hyuk-hee murmured, "No, but they die unexpectedly."

This really was a strange day. Oray walked over to them like a relief pitcher coming into the game. The Superman logo on his shirt bounced along to his steps. He pulled the man to one side and spoke to him in a hushed tone. Next, he beckoned the woman to his other side and said something to her, too.

"You think he got their votes?" Hyuk-hee asked.

"I don't know. He's only had experience with women voters."

"He must be working for the ruling party. He looks pleased with himself."

"Then I guess he won't win."

Oray gestured for us to come over. By now, it was completely dark, and all the passing cars had their lights on. The emergency lights issuing from the Volkswagen cast a blinking shadow on the pavement.

Oray patted me on the shoulder. "You have to go."

"Go where?"

Oray pointed to the man, who was pulling his motorcycle up from the ground.

"I told him you want to ride with him on his bike. He'll take you to Hengdang-dong, where he lives. I lied and said you live there, too."

144

I let out a low whistle.

"I told him we were trying to decide how to get you home since we don't live in the same area," he continued.

"So?"

"He thinks you were going to have to walk to Seoul. When I told him our predicament, he said he'd be happy to help. You're lucky."

"I *am* lucky. That bike's already been in an accident, so chances are it won't get into another. I'll be safe with him," I quipped.

"Find out where he lives," Oray instructed.

"Do I need to count how many spoons he has, too?"

"You don't have to go to his house. Just lie and give her a fake address. She'll believe it's where he lives."

"May I ask a question?"

"One."

"Why me?" The fact was that my body was the least suitable to ride on a motorcycle. "Besides, where will you be going?

"Amusement park," Hyuk-hee answered this time. "The magical place where time still travels but we don't age."

"And why do you get to go to an amusement park and not me?"

"Because, Apartment 303, you're her neighbor. It's your responsibility to help a neighbor in need."

"That's the only reason?"

"And she asked for two wishes and you're granting neither of them."

He had a point.

The street was dark and unfamiliar. I climbed behind the man on his motorcycle and grabbed him around the waist. The woman waved at me from her Volkswagen. It was too dark to make out her expression. She reminded me of an umpire calling an out. It seemed ominous somehow.

The woman drove off with her passengers, probably headed to the amusement park. After seeing the Volkswagen off, the man revved up his motorcycle. He turned to me, thinking I lived near his house.

"We'll probably arrive past eleven o'clock."

"Do you normally work this late?" I asked.

"I usually get off at eight but one of my customers needed an urgent delivery."

The motorcycle's engine sounded distinctly different from the car.

"Have you ever gotten back on your bike less than thirty minutes after an accident before?" I asked.

"Two years ago, I had an accident on this same bike. I hit a kid on a bicycle, but miraculously, the kid wasn't hurt. It was an act of God. That's when I decided that if something like that ever happened to me, I'd pay it forward. Today, I got my chance."

Two years earlier, he'd resolved that if he got into an accident, he'd walk away from it unharmed. We took off on the motorcycle.

"Where are your friends going?" he shouted over the roar of the engine.

"They're going to die!" I shouted.

"Anyone could keel over dead in this heat!" he yelled back. I merely nodded.

He voiced his concern that the woman's car, an imported vehicle, used too much gas. He didn't seem worried that his bike was using more because of my weight.

It was strange to know there were still good people in this world.

He wouldn't take no for an answer, so I had to accept his invitation to visit his home. It was a small house at the base of a low hill. He lived with his father, wife, and children, who all looked like him. When we entered the yard, they all came out to greet him. When he introduced me, they immediately ushered me into the living room and to a seat that seemed to be reserved for an honored guest. The man's wife brought small plates and a platter of watermelon. I sat there nodding and spitting watermelon seeds onto my plate as the man triumphantly recounted what transpired on the street. Finally, I was allowed to say goodbye and take my leave.

The man walked me out to the street. We bid each other farewell under the dim light of the one streetlamp. This was the first time I saw his face up close. He was sweating profusely. In the light, his face was pale and ashen. Dark shadows lingered beneath both eyes. I suddenly remembered the woman's ghostly wave as we left.

I walked for about fifteen minutes before spotting a bus. I got off downtown, where the streets were still heavy from the heat of the day. It was a languid summer night. A certain peaceful lull, like the lull that comes after a long, futile battle, hung in the air. Frustrated people were desperately trying to flag down cabs. A knot of young men were squatting outside a convenience store, lazily drinking beer. Drunk men staggered from a darkened alley like maggots crawling out of a roasted chestnut.

I wanted to kick a small stone but there was none to be found. I passed a man in a cart selling odd little dolls and pirated cassette tapes. Streetlamps stood spaced apart, separated by trees. I sat down on a stone bench. The pop song playing from the man's speaker ended abruptly, and was quickly followed by music from a band that left the business years ago. Oray once told me that after listening to shitty dance music all day, street vendors played their favorite songs before calling it a night.

I have more days ahead of me,
Why should I worry?
The pain is behind me now...

As I listened to the music, I glanced up at the huge electronic public service display board outside the Kyobo Building. *Work like an ant. Summer is fleeting.*

I turned to look at the news feed crawling across the bottom of the screen. One headline disappeared and was quickly followed by more.

In the song that was playing, the singer crooned that his troubles meant nothing to him anymore. I wondered if Oray and Hyuk-hee had seen the laser show at the theme park. Or if they'd gone on the rollercoaster.

Earlier that afternoon, Hyuk-hee told me a story. "One summer night, ten years ago, I was driving on the freeway with a girl next to me."

"Was she pretty? With long hair?"

"Yup, and she had legs that went on for miles. When she laughed, it sounded like she was biting into something sweet, and when she smiled, the birthmark on her cheek became more pronounced. Every time I said something, she erupted in nervous giggles, as if I'd felt her up. It always came on so suddenly, like when you accidentally blast your car horn you. Laughing, she'd move her arm—which was hairy, sticky, and for some reason, cold— closer to mine.

"In any case, she was a pretty girl, and her hair smelled nice. That night, after it got dark, we bought beer and peanuts and headed to a motel with AC. Once side, we saw that the back window was covered by heavy, dirty drapes. The girl refused to let me take off her skirt because she was scared of whatever was behind those drapes. In the end, I had to open them so she could see what was there."

"Wait, I think I know this one. The body of a woman who'd been killed two days earlier?" I asked.

"A rat and a cockroach fucking?" Oray chirped.

"A big bag stuffed with cash, with *Finders, keepers* written on it?" I shouted.

Hyuk-hee shook his head. "No."

"James Bond?" Oray tried.

"The woman from Apartment 304?"

"No."

"Then what?"

"The ocean."

Oray and I nodded in understanding. "That's terrifying."

I was about to tell them that was around the same time I'd gone to the beach with the two girls, but Hyuk-hee was faster. "Those days are gone, but happily, we still have our beer. Now, rock, paper, scissors."

Oray lost. He got up to buy beer.

A lion appeared in a cell phone ad on the electronic display board. I'd seen lions in a TV documentary. The narrator had droned, "These lions are exhausted. They have to consume 350 zebras every year. It's enough to overwhelm them unless the creatures have a strong will to live. The laws of nature are fatally cruel to those who depend on coincidence alone."

Suddenly a strong wind shook the tree branches. I thought of the story Oray's mother told him when he was young: When you see a tree shaking all of a sudden, it means someone you know has just died. The shaking happens when that person's ghost saw you, alighted briefly on a branch, then took off.

Instinctively, I looked up at the ticker news feed but saw no mention of a traffic accident. Nor was there any news of a rollercoaster suddenly malfunctioning, sending passengers plummeting to their deaths.

It was 00:00. Midnight. No one had died. The woman was indeed a LIAR.

It had been a long day. I wondered if mayflies said that before they died at the end of their one-day life—although it wouldn't really matter to them. The song from the speakers continued.

I have more days ahead of me,
Why worry?
Every day is a joy ..

In My Life

I heard this story from Hye-lin.

Hye-lin's real name was Jung-sook. After reading work by the writer Chun Hye-lin in high school, Jung-sook set two goals for herself: one, to become a writer and the other, to take on the pseudonym Chun Hye-lin. Although she didn't become a writer, she did succeed in changing her name. She owned a small, unpretentious bar called *In My Life*, where everyone knew her by that name. It was located on a street of small shops and cafés near Ewha Women's University.

Some customers noticed the book she kept next to her records—*And Then She Was Silent* by Chun Hye-lin—and assumed she was the writer. Hye-lin usually stayed curled up in her chair with her nose buried in her book, which perpetuated the notion that she was a thoughtful, contemplative person. Not one of these customers, who believed that reading was proof of a person's intellect, knew that the real author had killed herself some twenty years ago, and was therefore, silent.

As with most female bar owners, it was hard to determine Hye-lin's age. When she was hauling cases of beer or working the cash register, she looked as weary as a cafeteria lady at the end of a long shift, but the dreamy gaze that lingered on the rain outside her window couldn't have belonged to a woman older than thirty. When she was drinking with one of her regulars, her face held the mirthless sorrow of a madam who'd lost her lover a long time ago and was living a life of shadows, commiserating with forlorn strangers.

It seemed like Hye-lin kept the bar open not to make money but to have a place to sit. What she was most interested in were the stories that people told, not their money. I gathered from our late night conversations that she still dreamed of becoming a writer.

Her bar wasn't for adventure seekers or those who liked new things. People who were intimidated by new places or who hated to stand out found their way to the dimly lit corners of Hye-lin's bar. They always had a reliable listener in Hye-lin, to whom they told stories that no one else found interesting. Most of them appreciated not being obliged to order expensive food to go with their drinks. Other than these regular customers, Hye-lin's bar was almost always empty.

When I think back to those days, it seems unlikely that I, of all people, befriended Hye-lin and Zumi, the young girl who worked at the bar in exchange for free beer. Immediately after graduating from the women's university, I married a researcher at an institute staffed by quiet, nervous men in glasses. I was soon whisked away to a comfortable Gangnam apartment where I lived the cookie cutter life of a happy housewife. I didn't cling to an unfulfilled dream like Hye-lin did, and I didn't revel in the hedonistic pleasures of youth the way Zumi did.

When I brought the girls to my house, drunk, at two in the morning, my husband gingerly inched away from us, as if I were a housekeeper who'd come to the wrong house.

He hissed, "What's going on? I don't understand what you're doing."

If someone were to ask me what I was thinking at the time, I wouldn't be able to give a good answer. In those days, however, I often found myself suddenly dropping whatever I was doing in the kitchen, turning off the tap, grabbing two persimmons for Hye-lin, and rushing out the door to catch a cab to Sinchon. Or I'd come home from the supermarket and innocently begin arranging fresh chrysanthemums in a vase before glancing up at the setting sun, wrapping the flowers, and dashing off to see Hye-lin.

Only after taking a sip of the beer at her bar could I breathe a sigh of relief. Only then did the crippling anxiety leave me.

Hye-lin told me many stories—stories about the customers who frequented her café. I committed myself to these stories like a high school senior devouring her test prep lessons, and I was soon able to pick out similar patterns.

All the stories carried a hint of sadness. When I commented on this, Hye-lin smiled. "The stories I want to write are sad, too."

"When I was little," she continued, "my grandmother said that if I liked sad stories too much, I'd end up a poor woman. I still prefer them to other stories though."

Sometimes, I did the bulk of the talking, which was both surprising and oddly satisfying. Growing up, I was a quiet, composed child. Though I basked in the praise of the adults who remarked on my thoughtfulness and manners, I secretly yearned to be one of the chatterboxes, the girls who said whatever was on their minds. I envied their uninhibited speech, their carefree ways.

When I was with Hye-lin, I didn't have to prove myself. I could talk about anything I wanted. I talked about the teacher I had a crush on in high school, the silly dates I had in college, the pleasure I felt when my husband told me he knew he was going to marry me ten minutes into our first date. I talked about how loving and dedicated he was, and how I trusted him so much I didn't care that he was never at his desk when I called.

When I told Hye-lin these things, she furrowed her brow.

"I'll wake up tomorrow and not remember a thing you said," she scoffed.

"Why not?"

"Because there's nothing sad about them."

"What difference does that make?"

"I don't know." Closing her eyes, she gave the matter some thought. "There's nothing interesting in them."

"Nothing?"

Hye-lin was right. My life contained nothing that was pure or raw, nothing with a beating heart. It was almost as if I weren't alive.

The more I drank, the better I got at it. Drinking invigorated me. With alohol's help, I could let go of my stuffy personality and finally start living my life.

I took to observing what went on at the bar. At the first sign of any trouble, I rushed to where the action was. I listened hard whenever an argument broke out. When a man and woman entered together, I observed their body language to guess which one was the slave and which the master. I screamed the lyrics to Deep Purple's "Highway Star," jumping up and down and tossing my head. I squinted at the writing on the walls in the bathroom: *I was bored so I went to a friend's house where I found only his sister.* Past midnight, I was often found staggering down the street looping arms with Hye-lin, kicking every trash bag in sight.

I thought that if there were a place on Earth where I lived my real life, it was In My Life.

I first stumbled upon In My Life one autumn day five years ago, just as the sun was setting. My third attempt at in vitro fertilization had failed and I'd spent the previous two days in bed. Realizing I had to get a grip on myself, I decided to formulate a plan to get my life back in order. First, I'd get my hair permed. I went to the area near Ewha University, where all the good salons were. I left the salon searching for the next thing to do. I found a telephone booth and called my husband's office. As usual, he wasn't there.

The sun was setting. Housewives were fretting in their kitchens over what to cook for dinner. Outside the university, young girls in colorful patterned dresses spilled out into the streets as if someone had emptied a sack of them. I stared dumbfounded as they breezed past on the neon-lit streets. I felt lost. I stayed a long time in that telephone booth—God knows why— before I looked up and noticed a sign across the street. In My Life. I slowly made my way there.

In My Life was on the third floor of the building. Rounding the second flight of stairs, I began to regret heading there, and when I opened the door to a tiny, wretched little dump, I felt even worse. The straight-haired lady reading behind the bar uttered *Hello* in a tired, bored voice. I had a cup of coffee and left. Climbing down the stairs, I didn't think I'd ever come back again.

I also didn't think I'd need another perm for a while, but about a month later, I was listening to the radio when I decided to head to Sinchon for another hairstyle change.

I arrived late in the afternoon, so by the time I got my curls, it was dark. Out in the street, I was momentarily struck by the confusing mess of city lights around me. I turned and made my way to the subway station. I passed the telephone booth but didn't stop.

My feet took me to a theater on a street corner. It was as if I'd come to Sinchon for this very theater. After purchasing a ticket, I looked up to see the movie was *Susan Brink's Arirang*, starring one of the most popular actresses at the time. It was boring, but I stayed inside the nearly empty theater until the end, sobbing loudly.

By the time I left the theater, it was very late. I had a cheeseburger and Coke at a fast food restaurant, then walked out and leaned against the glass entrance. Where to now?

The street was still swollen with people refusing to go home. Their longing and desire gave off a rotten stench. There are two ways to spend the night. Either you stay at home looking out at the street or you spend it in the street looking for your way home. The calm of the dead. The exuberance of the rotting.

Ducking into a crowded bar, I asked the young, frazzled waitress for the simplest things on the menu, beer and French fries. When they arrived, I stared at the foam clinging to the sides of the mug, then stabbed at the slender French fries with a fork until it dawned on me that I didn't belong in that bar.

It began to rain. The waitress brought the check. "We're about to close."

Outside, the street was dark as a cave. I gingerly stepped into the darkness, like a traveler about to set sail on unfamiliar seas. I walked in the rain, passing how many crosswalks I don't remember. I walked past an overpass then retraced my steps. Trains roared by, blasting their horns. I lurched dizzily toward any glimpse of light, like a desert wanderer dragged along by a phantom he confuses for a mirage. By then I was thoroughly drenched from the rain, but I had nowhere to go. There was no one to welcome me in this street of the dead.

The only reason I knocked, shivering, on the door of In My Life was because I'd been there once before. I felt a wave of relief when I saw the bar, but its door was grimly shut. No light came from within, not even a faint one. I knocked softly on the door but no one came. I realized this was the end. I had nowhere else to go. Feeling my legs give way, I slumped against the door like a sack of potatoes. Just then, as if by magic, the door slid open. Inside was a whole other world. There were lights and people singing around a woodstove. Dazed, I stood there transfixed like that boy in the fairy tale who chances upon a magical festival that only comes once every thousand years. As I stood there, a man who was strumming a guitar turned to face me. I felt a sudden jolt. The expression on his face reminded me of something I'd long forgotten—the look of a man with real presence.

"I didn't know the door was unlocked," remarked the owner, approaching where I stood in the dark. Her voice was sharp. "Business hours are over. We're closed."

Desperately, I pushed the door open, as if to prove I belonged there. When I stepped into the light, everyone saw I was soaked through. The owner stared at my face hard, then finally relented. "Come in. It's warm inside."

Later, Hye-lin explained that she let me in because I had a sad look about me.

"We don't normally sing here, but when that customer started playing the guitar, everyone began singing along. Sometimes, after we close for the night, we draw the curtains and sing together for hours. I'm always nervous the authorities might hear us and close us down."

The customer playing the guitar was the man I'd seen that first night.

Hye-lin later confided, "Since he stopped coming, this place has been so empty. Even the regulars aren't coming as often as they did. Business was never great, but we still had it good when he was here."

Then she proceeded to tell me his story. There were other, more eccentric and interesting stories, but the story of this man made the strongest impression on me. It's a story that's common enough, and yet I'm certain it's the only love story of its kind.

We go through many loves in our lives, and they spawn many stories. The only time a love feels unique and extraordinary is when it's happening. Love in its present progressive state. I say that his story seemed to be the only love story there ever was because I saw myself in it.

Let me tell you his story. Given how it's been years since those carefree days with Hye-lin, I can only hope to do it justice.

Hye-lin hated riots and protests. She usually opened the bar at two or three in the afternoon, which, for her, was when the day began. She frowned each time the smell of tear gas fought its way into the bar when she opened the windows to let out the dust.

That day, like any other, she came to work at three in the afternoon. Turning her key in the lock, she pushed the door open and was immediately assaulted by the sour smell of last night's beers in the damp trapped air. Coughing, she opened the windows. After giving a quick sweep of the place, she immediately closed them again. She'd glanced outside and spied suspicious activity near the university gates. Soon, the street filled with commotion and noise.

No one showed up even after three plays of Sade's "Smooth Operator" on the turntable. Hye-lin was reading, her chin propped on one hand and the other lazily stirring a cup of cold coffee. Just then, there was a bang at the door and someone shoved it open, creating ripples on her coffee. In walked a man, surrounded by a cloud of tear gas.

He'd only been rough with the door because he thought it would be much heavier, an honest mistake given how thick it looks. Sheepishly, he made his way as quietly as possible to a seat by the window. Hye-lin brought over the menu. As she did, she sneezed. The man immediately shook the dust from his shoulder, which only made things worse. Hye-lin headed to the bar to fetch the two beers he'd asked for. There, she surreptitiously wiped her tears with a towel.

When she came back with the beers, the man asked, "Is this place named after the Beatles song?"

"I don't know." Hye-lin admitted to keeping the name the former owner had given the bar. At that, the man looked crestfallen.

"Would you mind playing that song for me if you have it?"

Hye-lin managed to find the dusty Beatles album in an old box of records. "In My Life" was the eleventh track on the band's *Rubber Soul* album.

The man stared out the window as he listened to the music. Taking a small notebook from his pocket, he began to write. He seemed immersed in what he was doing, stopping to reach for his beer only after filling several pages. Noticing the fountain pen in his hand, Hye-lin wondered if he was a novelist. She didn't take her eyes off him until he finally looked up from his writing, saw that it had gone dark outside, and got up from his seat, leaving a half-full glass of beer behind.

He was quite tall, with an oval face and a shock of hair that fell across his forehead, lending him a certain boyishness. But the fingers on his left hand, which he used to dig in his wallet for the money, were rough with calluses. As Hye-lin counted out the change, sneaking a few furtive glances his way, he looked around the room in embarrassed silence. Suddenly, his eyes fell on something. He squinted. It was a guitar, occupying one corner of the bar.

"Is that guitar usable?" he asked with suppressed excitement.

"I don't know. I only put it there to spice up the décor."

It was, in fact, Zumi who'd brought the ancient guitar. Hye-lin felt uncomfortable any time a customer asked about it, but the man had already walked over, picked it up, and begun tuning it in earnest. The strings shivered under his touch, finally allowed to stretch themselves and sing.

Hye-lin was surprised the guitar was still capable of music. She narrowed her eyes and watched as he expertly shifted it to one shoulder. He stroked the guitar lovingly. Hye-lin lowered the volume on the music to encourage him to play, but he gently laid the instrument on the floor. Then he left, just as boisterously as he'd come in. The flimsy door, held together with nothing more than a few pieces of plywood, shook in his wake. Hye-lin felt somehow abandoned. She was about to put the guitar back in its place when she saw the coating of dust on it, so thick the man's fingerprints had left obvious imprints. She was about to wipe it down with a wet rag, when she felt a faint warmth from the cold metal strings.

A week or two later, the man returned. He was with a woman, and they were clearly drunk. The woman, obviously unmarried, was clearly in love with him. She nestled up to him, pouring his drinks and shelling the peanuts for easy snacking. She angled her body coquettishly and looked longingly into his eyes.

She laughed often, and every time she did, the man smiled, but his heart wasn't in it. He was looking at her, but he wasn't seeing her. Instead, his eyes looked past her toward the corner where a big potted plant stood. Hye-lin knew he was looking for the guitar.

The woman staggered to the bar. "May I use your phone?"

As Hye-lin pushed the phone toward her, she saw it was past eleven o'-clock.

"Yeah, it's me. Did I keep you waiting?" the woman spoke into the phone. "Sorry about that. Want to come out? I'm with someone, if that's okay. What? You'll come? Isn't your husband coming home soon? Are you sure? Okay then... Let me give you the address."

She frowned and pursed her lips. She was annoyed her friend was insisting on joining them.

The friend arrived not much later. Hye-lin recognized her immediately. With her waif-like body and huge, frightened eyes set into a pale, porcelain face, she looked like the heroine in a sad love story Hye-lin meant to write someday. She blinked slowly, letting her eyes adjust to the darkness. Upon discovering her friend, she gave a faint glimmer of a smile. Her smile caught at Hye-lin's heart the way the man's gaze did when it alighted hungrily on the guitar.

The friend sat down next to the woman and nodded quietly at the man. She didn't look straight at him.

The man offered her a glass of beer. Flustered, she quickly reached for it with both hands, accidentally catching the end of the table runner and almost knocking the bottles over. Frantically, she reached out to grab them. As she did, the glass in her other hand spilled beer over the table. The man made to steady the glass, and accidentally grazed her hand with his. Flinching, she withdrew her arm, splashing beer in his face.

"What did you do?" the woman shrieked. Hye-lin ran over with napkins, and saw that the friend was trembling. Slowly, the man wiped the beer from his face. Hye-lin saw that he was staring straight at the woman.

Later, the man picked up the guitar. As he tuned it, the woman quivered with anticipation. Meanwhile, her friend was looking out the window, sipping from her glass.

At first, he sang the woman's requests, mostly songs from the top of the pop charts. He was good, no doubt about it, but his singing sounded dry, void of emotion. When the woman started singing along, he stopped his singing entirely, merely accompanying her on the guitar. In the end, she finished most of the songs herself. She was a good singer, too, but Hye-lin was getting bored. She'd expected something more from the man. Thinking he was done with the guitar, she got up to put another record on the turntable. Just then, he started singing "In My Life." "There are places I remember..."

His voice was mellow and crisp, and as lonely as a walk on an autumn day. Hye-lin was gripped with an overpowering sadness. When the song ended, she closed her eyes to hold on to the lingering words of the chorus, but the woman's loud clapping rudely snapped her from her reverie.

Rather than trying to appreciate the memories that could have inspired such feeling, the woman whooped like a fan at a baseball stadium and hollered out more song requests. Hye-lin frowned and thought she needed to be married off to a boring man, have his boring children, and have to attend boring kindergarten parties.

Hye-lin hoped the man wouldn't play the requested songs. She was ruining everything. In the story Hye-lin hoped to write, the characters needed to be sad, or failing that, have at least a measure of elegance.

"Hey, are you crying?"

At the woman's question, Hye-lin looked up at the friend, whose face was buried in her hands. She was still as a statue, her bone-white fingers covering her face.

"What's wrong? Why are you crying?" The woman rushed over to her.

157

The friend leaned against her shoulder. The woman put her arm around her friend, accidentally loosening the friend's blouse and revealing her delicate collarbones.

The friend didn't say a word, as if asking her why she was crying was like asking her why she didn't cry sooner, as if her tears were justified and needed no explanation. Hye-lin understood. After all, sadness has a certain instinctive quality to it. She pitied the woman who was badgering the poor friend with questions. Apparently, she didn't get it. Hye-lin turned to her beer and slowly poured it into a glass. The man was doing the same.

Hye-lin placed a record on the turntable. The friend was still crying, and the man was silently drinking his beer. The woman was quiet, too, for once. There was no one else at the bar. The four of them owned the night's sadness.

About a month later, the woman and her friend came back. They were with a man, and Hye-lin could tell from where he sat that he was the friend's husband. Their flushed faces betrayed the fact this wasn't their first bar of the night. The husband looked around the bar.

"This place is nice, Honey. I'm impressed you drink in places like this."

The woman guffawed, "Thanks to yours truly!"

At that, the husband laughed. "Take her out more often. If you didn't, she'd never leave the house. She's always been shy, even when we were dating."

He looked adoringly at his wife. She smiled back at him with the awareness that she was loved.

Hye-lin felt rage, for some reason. When the woman approached the bar asking to use the phone, she practically threw it at her.

She placed a phone call every ten minutes or so, possibly motivated by the picture of domestic bliss in front of her. But each time she did, she slammed the phone down and walked away muttering, "Where is he? Why hasn't he come home yet? What's keeping him?" When Hye-lin saw her returning to the bar after a half dozen beers, she automatically pushed the phone toward her. Again, there was no answer on the other end. She turned to Hye-lin.

"Do you have any congratulatory music you can play for us?"

"I'm sorry?"

"My friend's celebrating her wedding anniversary today. Maybe you can play some sort of congratulatory song?"

Smiling awkwardly, Hye-lin replied, "I'm sorry but I don't think we carry that kind of music."

The woman then asked if she could borrow the guitar. That reminded Hye-lin of the man who sang "In My Life." She glanced at the guitar, which was propped weakly against a corner like a bride who'd broken her vow of chastity.

Unfortunately, the husband couldn't play guitar. The woman was disappointed that she didn't get to show off her singing skills and aggrieved that her man wasn't there to accompany her. She started drinking furiously. She burst out laughing at every one of the husband's lame jokes. Clearly, she was drunk.

The husband was outgoing and cheerful, cracking jokes with the woman and just as easily steering the conversation toward his wife so she wouldn't feel excluded. He was charming and funny, as if his life depended on pleasing the two women. Laughing uproariously, he seemed to demonstrate how to properly enjoy oneself at a bar.

After dealing with scores of customers, Hye-lin could tell this man's job involved meeting with clients, an occupation that demanded much wining and dining of potential buyers. Hye-lin surmised this was a man who could quite easily sleep with a call girl for the sake of business and just as easily pick up a bouquet of flowers on the way home to his wife, the hooker's smell still on his suit.

The woman looked on contentedly as her husband and the woman chatted away, carefully plucking a stray hair from the back of her husband's shirt. Untying the scarf she must have received as an anniversary present that morning, she tied it another way around her neck. She didn't seem at all fragile or frightened. Rather, she was like a small, pretty seashell proudly displayed by her husband in a big box. Inside, though, the shell was empty.

What made her cry the other night? Hye-lin turned to look out at the dark October sky. She wasn't interested in tears that weren't sad.

The woman cried again a few days later.

That evening, the woman walked in with the man who'd played the guitar. Hye-lin yawned, no longer interested. About an hour later, the man's overcast expression suddenly brightened when he glanced up at the doorway. Noticing this, Hye-lin turned to see who it was. It was the friend. She was wearing the same olive green blouse she'd worn the night she came with her husband but without the scarf, the absence of which accentuated her long, white neck. Smoothing her hair behind one ear, she smiled softly. In that moment, any man would have felt the urge to run over and take her in his arms.

They talked merrily over drinks. The man played the guitar again, and again, she sobbed. They were the last customers of the night. After they left, Hye-lin was clearing their table when she looked out the window and saw it was raining. The man was soaking wet and attempting to hail a cab, the two women huddled behind him. Dead leaves had been swept by the rain into cheerless, soggy piles on the sidewalk. *After the rain, a crisp chill will no doubt descend upon the city,* Hye-lin thought. She considered watching until they left but changed her mind and carried the tray of beer bottles to the bar. She turned off the lights and climbed down the stairs. When she looked outside again, they were gone.

They came back a few times after that, always sitting in the same arrangement, drinking in the same order. The only change was that she stopped crying. Instead, the sobbing was replaced by constant deep sighs that she took care not to let the man notice. When the woman was in the restroom, they fell into an awkward silence. When she returned, they fidgeted nervously, hoping the awkwardness wasn't too apparent.

One day, Hye-lin realized the man hadn't sung in a while and that it coincided with when she'd stopped crying. The only reason she didn't cry anymore was because he'd stopped singing.

Often, Hye-lin noticed it was raining on the nights they came. *It's raining so much this autumn,* she thought to herself.

Sometimes, the woman showed up alone. When she did, she always called the man, who never came. Slowly, the woman confided in Hye-lin her feelings for the man, how she and her friend had gone to the same high school, how abandoned she felt whenever the man refused to come out. Not much of this was new information to Hye-lin. The only thing that surprised her was that the man wasn't a writer but employed at a travel agency housed in the same building where the woman worked as a secretary.

One other thing Hye-lin hadn't guessed was that the man had wanted to become a musician. When he was sixteen, he first heard the music of the Beatles, which inspired him to do two things: one, to become a singer, and two, to go to Liverpool, where John Lennon was born. He'd been to Liverpool twice already, but he hadn't made it as a musician. In his free time, he still liked to write music but he hadn't played the guitar in years, according

160

to the woman.

"I grew up in an average family," she once confessed. "I was only an average student. I had average looks. Everything in my life was average. I had no complaints though. I wasn't planning on becoming someone or achieving something. I was just passing the time. When I first met him, I realized that I had no dreams. I envy him for having one. It doesn't matter that his dream might be impossible to reach. When you have a dream, it makes you come alive. It's almost as if it gives your life reason."

One evening, the bar was bustling with uncharacteristic activity. One of the regulars, an industrial designer, had brought two friends along for his birthday. A lighting director and his girlfriend, both regular customers, offered to throw him a party. The lighting director's girlfriend was about to dash out to pick up a birthday cake when another regular customer, a tennis instructor, walked in. After being filled in, he insisted he'd get the champagne. The bar was throbbing with excitement.

Most of the regulars knew one another, so it wasn't unusual for them to hang out together. Hye-lin helped to grease the wheels a bit, too. She was running to and fro with the preparations when the phone rang. At first, Hye-lin couldn't place the female voice.

"I'm sorry, who is this?"

"Hye-lin, it's me, I..."

Fortunately, her faltering voice brought to Hye-lin's mind those large, woeful black eyes. The woman asked if the man who played the guitar was at there.

"No, he's not here right now. Why? Did you make plans?" Hye-lin asked.

"No, no!" she stammered indignantly, as if she were being grilled by a detective who was accusing her of adultery. "No, I only wanted to know if he was there. Are you sure he's not?"

"He's not here."

"He's not?"

"..."

"Okay... I'll be there soon."

She added that she needed a drink to clear her head but she didn't want to come if the man was there. Either she was uncomfortable with the idea of them drinking together or fearful of what might happen. Hye-lin reassured her that the man hadn't come by himself in a long time. In fact, she added that they were throwing a birthday party for another customer and that the woman should feel free to stop by. The woman hesitated before hanging up. Just then, the customer charged with buying the cake came back, and Hye-lin hurried to the kitchen to retrieve some plates. She didn't see the man walk in and take a seat by the corner.

Only after singing happy birthday and popping the champagne did Hye-lin noticed the solitary figure. Approaching him, she nervously glanced at the door before she asked, "What brings you here by yourself tonight?"

He smiled and remarked on the festivities that were going on. He said he felt like having a drink. Hye-lin was about to blurt out the woman had said the same thing before thinking better of it.

Hye-lin felt her heart pounding as she kept looking at the door. She debated waiting by the stairs until the woman showed up to warn her that he was inside, but she also believed that coincidences are masked enablers of fate. If it's written in the stars that they're to meet tonight, nothing could prevent that from happening. He might see her on the stairs, or they might bump into each other on the street.

As soon as she walked in, they saw one another. It was as Hye-lin predicted. The woman stood rooted to her spot. She didn't want to sit at his table but it would look strange if she sat anywhere else. If the man hadn't waved at her at that exact moment, her big eyes would have brimmed over with tears.

Avoiding each other's gaze, they drank beers together. But as time passed, their expressions softened and their eyes shined with a glow that seemed to be lit from the inside. When the man picked up the guitar, her shoulders shook. For the second time he sang "In My Life" in the bar.

"But of all these friends and lovers..."

As he sang the last verse, he lifted his eyes and looked straight into hers. This time, she didn't avoid his gaze.

When the song ended, the other customers applauded. The lighting director's girlfriend was particularly ecstatic, and the designer's two friends shouted for an encore. The man obliged them. Soon, they were all singing together. Everyone was drunk. The lighting director's girlfriend sighed, "You make such a lovely couple."

The man and woman looked at each other and smiled. Their smiles held the confidence that fate was on their side.

The man sang, locking his eyes with the hers. The warmth from his eyes transferred to hers, which shone beautifully. His eyes were bringing her back from the dead, the way the prince woke Sleeping Beauty with his kiss.

What's her name? Hye-lin wondered. She imagined that the woman probably had a unique, beautiful name. As they walked out hand-in-hand into the night, Hye-lin thought about asking her, but decided not to. That was for him to do.

For a while, none of them appeared. Instead, her husband began showing up, always with a loud group of drunken people. They discussed boring stuff—work, current events, women—in the loudest, most obnoxious voices possible. When they arrived, the quiet bar transformed into a raucous back-alley pub. To Hye-lin, who was more interested in stories than money, they were a contemptuous breed indeed.

They were repugnant in other ways, too. Whenever Hye-lin came over with the drinks, the husband grabbed her roughly by the wrist and suggested she join them. When she coldly refused, he sneered at her for acting like a stuck up bitch. He was the kind of person Hye-lin absolutely abhorred, the type of man who had dreams and wasn't given to behaving in any classy way. He even lacked the ruddy honesty of his wife's friend.

The more she studied the husband, the more Hye-lin found herself hoping that the woman knew no happiness with him. If she needed this man's love to be happy, she no longer belonged in Hye-lin's novel. It would be a crime for this woman to love her husband. She should only love the man with the guitar. Staying in a loveless marriage is immoral and goes against the beauty of nature.

Hye-lin watched the woman's husband become more and more drunk. There were no other customers save the lighting director's girlfriend, who was here by herself. Zumi had also come to help and was wiping the refrigerator door.

When the man who'd played the guitar walked in, Hye-lin was pleased to see him

"Hello!"

When she asked after him, he replied that the woman was meeting him. He headed to his customary table. Why was he meeting the woman, and not her friend? Hye-lin suddenly remembered that the friend's husband was sitting at the next table. Her heart leaped to her throat.

The man looked gloomy, his footsteps heavy. He was walking to his table when he accidentally bumped into the husband's chair. The husband, clearly drunk, glared at him. Without turning to look at him, the man murmured an apology and sat at his table. The husband looked like he was about to say something before he turned away. Hye-lin swallowed hard.

Drunk people get into fights over the silliest things, especially in places like this. The previous week, a fight had broken out in a downstairs café involving two men fighting over a woman. They swung at each other with broken beer bottles, one of which cut the woman's face. Their fight was also over almost nothing. One of the men had suggested they order three more beers, but the woman said they should just order one more. When the other man seconded the woman's opinion, the first guy leaped to his feet in outrage.

Hye-lin nervously eyed the group sitting with the husband as she brought a few beers to the man. One of them shouted for two more beers. Hye-lin looked around for Zumi and motioned for her to get the beers to them. She then sat down at the man's table.

"Why haven't you come in lately?"

"I was occupied with other things."

"You don't look well."

The man gave a wan smile.

There were grumblings heard from the husband's table that Hye-lin was playing favorites with her paying customers. Suddenly, Hye-lin heard Zumi cry out, "Let go of me! I'm a waitress, not a hostess!"

"What did you say?" one of the men glowered.

Hye-lin jumped to her feet, but she was too late. The sound of broken glass pierced the air.

"You can't talk to me like that, you cunt!" The men had grabbed Zumi by the hair. They were all terribly drunk. Hye-lin ran over.

"Sir, please! Let her go!"

Hye-lin pleaded with them to stop, but the men only laughed. "Is this how you treat your customers? Is this how you run your business?"

"I'm so sorry. She's young, so she didn't know… Please let her go."

"Hye-lin! Help!" Zumi shrieked.

Out of the corner of her eye, Hye-lin saw the man get to his feet. She knew the fight would spiral out of control if he got involved. Hye-lin wasn't interested in justice; she didn't want any sort of drama. Releasing her grip on Zumi, she stopped the man from getting any closer.

"Please, don't do anything. They're just drunk," she whispered desperately.

But the man refused to stand back. It almost looked like he was eager for a fight.

"Let her go," he demanded in a low voice.

"Who the fuck are you? What do you want?" the woman's husband growled.

Suddenly, Hye-lin thought that maybe she should let them go at it. The same fate that brought the man and woman together that night must be at work here. Besides, they were standing in In My Life. Anywhere else, they were free to mingle with other people, but at least this was a place for the sad dreamers of the city.

She changed her mind when she saw the fire in their eyes. Victims of fate, they were filled with an inexplicable hatred that neither of them could place. Just then, the woman's friend walked in.

She quickly figured out what was going on and rushed to introduce them to each other. Upon being told that the man was the boyfriend of his wife's friend, his face relaxed into a grin and he offered his hand. But upon learning his opponent was the husband of the woman he loved, the man's expression grew darker. He refused to shake the husband's hand.

The woman dragged him out of the bar. As they passed the husband's table, the man clenched his fist. The men drew in their breath. But the man turned to a potted plant next to the table and shattered it with his fist. Hye-lin was the only one who knew that it was his own tragic love, and not the plant, that he had crushed. He staggered unevenly down the stairs.

The husband and his friends left not long after, leaving only the lighting director's girlfriend and Zumi, who was combing her disheveled hair. It was quiet. The girls were giggling that the man was like a white knight.

The man came back only once after that. It was raining the night he came. He sat alone, drinking past midnight, before grabbing the guitar again. Some of the regular customers politely turned to hear his music. When the lighting director's girlfriend, who was there by herself again that night, went to his table, the others joined in, forming a semi-circle around the woodstove. The man struck up "In My Life" for the third time.

"In my life I love you more..."

As the song was ending, the door suddenly slid open. The man was the first to notice. His eyes filled with hopeful longing. A woman, soaked from the rain, was standing in the doorway. Hye-lin approached and said, "We're closed."

Suddenly, the woman took a step closer, as if to prove she wasn't a stranger here. That's the first time I walked into "In My Life." The man stopped coming after that, all through autumn and winter.

The woman's husband, however, visited irregularly, always with a loud group of people. Once, when he'd gone to the restroom, his group began discussing him.

"Did he get divorced?" one of them asked.

"Bad news travels fast," another person replied. "He's not divorced, but his wife is staying with her parents. She's demanding a divorce, claiming she's pregnant with another man's child."

"Really? Is she going to marry the other guy?"

"I don't think so. She wants to raise the kid on her own. She begged and screamed, but it later turned out that she wasn't pregnant at all. He said he worried that he might drag her to a mental hospital if she stayed with him, so he made her stay with her parents."

When the man returned, they stopped talking. Hye-lin poured herself a glass of beer.

Not long after that, Hye-lin received a wedding invitation from the lighting director's girlfriend. Giggling, the girlfriend whispered, "You wouldn't recognize the groom from his name, but you know who he is. Want a hint? Birthday party, guitar, and the Beatles' 'In My Life'!" She burst out laughing. "We've been dating for two months. You never guessed, did you?"

Hye-lin didn't go to the wedding. She knew better than that. She knew she had no place in the real lives of her customers.

Hye-lin wanted to believe that the pale woman would come back. In fact, she waited for her. She wanted to offer her a drink and tell her the sad stories she'd heard over the years. Hye-lin thought the woman could benefit from the experience. But she never came.

"One more thing," Hye-lin added, after her story ended.

"Yes?"

"This is about someone else, a customer who always told the same story whenever she got drunk. She was a beautiful woman, with long curly hair. She looked nothing like the pale woman, but they had the same aura."

"Did they both look sad?" I wondered.

"Maybe that was it. Every time she got drunk, she took off her shoes and brought her knees up to her chest. She started murmuring to herself, with one hand over her knees and the other on her chin."

"Her eyes glazed over and became like empty marbles. She murmured, 'When I'm drunk, I call him. He always answers the phone. Realizing I'm drunk, he always comes for me. We drink in silence, for hours. The only time we speak is when we ask for more drinks. When midnight comes, we abruptly get up to leave, like a couple of Cinderellas. That's when he asks, *Why did you leave me?* I retort, 'You left, not me.' Angrily, he shouts back, *How can you accuse me of leaving? I bought you a ring!* Not backing down, I scream, 'Yeah? Where's that ring now? Who's wearing it? It's on someone else's hand! She's the one you chose!' By then, I'd be sobbing. He'd grab me by the shoulders and, swallowing hard, whisper, *Tell me you want it, and that ring is yours. If you want to, we can go back and make things right.* Before he finished, I'd shriek, 'Why didn't you say this before? Why did you leave me?' He'd shout back, *You're the one who was scared! My feelings for you never changed! I'm fucking helpless!* He'd be screaming by this time, too, but my screams would drown him out. 'Yeah? If that's true, prove it! Run away with me! Or let's both kill ourselves! Can you do that? Can you? See? You're lying! Did you think you could trick me again?' I'd start panting, hard. Pulling me close, he'd whisper, *Let's do it. Let's kill ourselves.* I'd whimper in his arms like a weak baby. Slowly, he'd guide me to the street and put me in a cab home. When I turned around, I'd see he was already gone. This happened every time we met. Weeks, months, years later, when I called him again, he picked up before the third ring. *It's you, isn't it? Is it you?*

Shaking her head, Hye-lin said, "My customers all seem the same. They only seem alive when they're sad."

I added, "Maybe we're only truly ourselves when we're sad. That's why we try so hard to get to that place."

Hye-lin nodded. "To feel alive."

It was a few days before Christmas and the streets of Sinchon were electric with activity. Burdened down with shopping bags and a freshly permed head of hair, I was stepping out to the street when I felt a cold, soft sensation on my cheek. Without warning, heavy snow began to fall. Everyone stopped in their tracks to look up and emit a collective sigh.

I ducked into a phone booth. My husband was at his desk. "I can meet you in an hour," he told me. "Do you want to wait somewhere?"

167

Through the frosted glass, I scanned the signboards across the street and noticed a white acrylic board with thick, red lettering. *Détente.* I told my husband where I'd be and hung up, but I suddenly realized I didn't want to go to *Détente.* The snow was falling with dogged purpose, like a woman's sworn promise to forget.

Five years earlier, I'd been in this very same booth. It was autumn, and dead leaves were detaching themselves from graying branches. I'd hurried into the booth to escape a sudden wave of emptiness. What I saw then was not the big glaring words of *Détente* but a smaller sign in the corner. On it was written in uncertain handwriting, *In My Life.*

The Author

Eun Heekyung was born in 1959 in Gochang County, Jeollabuk-do, Korea. She took a literature degree at Sookmyung Women's University, and a graduate degree in literature from Yonsei University, both in Seoul. She is the author of thirteen books of fiction, including the short story collections *To Try Talking with a Stranger* (1996), *Inheritance* (2002), *Beauty Looks Down on Me* (2007), *Like No Other* (2014); and the novels *Save the Last Dance for Me* (1998), *Secrets and Lies* (2005), *Let Boys Cry* (2010), and *Gesture Life* (2012). Her work has been translated into seven languages and won numerous awards, including the inaugural Munhakdongne Novel Award for her 1995 novel, *Gift From a Bird*; the Dongseo Literature Award, the Yi Sang Literary Award, the Korean Literature Award, and the Dong-in Literary Award

The Translator

Amber Hyun Jung Kim is a freelance translator and conference interpreter. Based in Seoul, she teaches at Hankuk University of Foreign Studies and is a Literature Translation Institute of Korea grant recipient. As a Korean-English simultaneous interpreter, she interprets for the Korean government, the European Parliament, and the private sector.

NOTES ON THE STORIES

"An Obviously Immoral Love"

Kimchi is a traditional fermented Korean side dish made of vegetables with a variety of seasonings.

Vouloir, c'est pouvoir - Where there's a will, there's a way.

Mt. Odae is a mountain peak in Gangwon, South Korea. At an elevation of 5,128 ft., it is the centerpiece of Odaesan National Park.

"Bruise"

Sashimi is a Japanese delicacy consisting of very fresh raw meat or fish sliced into thin pieces.

Soju is the best known liquor from Korea. It is distilled, vodka-like, rice liquor with high potency.

Sake is a Japanese rice wine.

Udon is a type of thick wheat flour noodle of Japanese cuisine.

"No One Checks the Time When They're Happy"

Jang-hung, located in South Jeolla Province in South Korea's southeastern tip, was designated as Asia's first "slow city" in 2007. It is famous for its production of shiitake mushrooms.

Changkyung Palace is a palace located in Seoul, South Korea. Built in the mid-15th century and originally the Summer Palace of the Goryeo King, it later became one of the Five Grand Palaces of the Joseon Dynasty.

Hanbok is the traditional Korean dress. It is often characterized by vibrant colors and simple lines without pockets.

Kumho-dong, Bongchun-dong, Shillim-dong, Shindang-dong, and Ahyun-dong are all neighborhoods in Seoul.

Seodaemun is a district located in northwestern Seoul.

"The Age of Lyricism"

Jean-Paul *Sartre* (June 21, 1905 – April 15, 1980) was a French philosopher, playwright, novelist, political activist, biographer, and literary critic. He was one of the key figures in the philosophy of existentialism and phenomenology, and one of the leading figures in 20th-century French philosophy and Marxism.

Carl Hilty (February 28, 1833 – October 12, 1909) was a Swiss philosopher, writer and lawyer. He famously said "Peace is only a hair's breadth away from war."

Thomas Wolfe (October 3, 1900 – September 15, 1938) was an American novelist of the early twentieth century.

Jeonju is the capital of North Jeolla province, South Korea.

Zhuge Liang (181 – 234), was a chancellor of the state of Shu Han during the Three Kingdoms period (188–280). He is recognized as the greatest and most accomplished strategist of his era, and has been compared to another great ancient Chinese strategist, Sun Tzu. His exploits are recounted in *The Romance of the Three Kingdoms*, a 14th-century Chinese epic novel about the century of war, turmoil, and bloodshed, written by Luo Guanzhong. It is considered one of the "Four Great Classical Novels" of Chinese literature. This epic is renowned for its beautiful style, complex and heroic characters, and enduring motifs and themes that remain relevant even in modern society. It not only left its influence throughout the Chinese culture, language, and literature, but also spawned many, many derivative works in various media throughout the world.

Kim Dae-jung (January 6, 1924 – August 18, 2009) was the eighth President of South Korea from 1998 to 2003, and recipient of the 2000 Nobel Peace Prize. He was sometimes referred to as the "Nelson Mandela of Asia."

The *East Sea*, also known as the Sea of Japan, is a marginal sea between the Korean Peninsula, Russia and the Japanese archipelago.

Busan is South Korea's second largest city after Seoul, with a population of approximately 3.6 million. The city is located on the southeastern-most tip of the Korean peninsula.

Jeju Island is a tropical island off the southern coast of South Korea, in the Korea Strait.

The *Gangnam* District is one of the twenty-five districts that make up the city of Seoul, South Korea. *Gangnam* literally means "South of the River." Widely known for its heavily concentrated wealth and high standard of living, as of the 2010 census, it had a population of 527,641, making it the fourth most populated district in Seoul.

"The Other Side of the World"

Namdaemun Market is a large traditional market in Seoul, South Korea. The market is located next to Namdaemun, the "Great South Gate," which was the main southern gate to the old city. It is the oldest and largest market in Korea.

Iguazu Falls is taller than Niagara Falls and twice as wide with 275 cascades spread in a horse-shoe shape over nearly two miles of the Iguazu River on the border between Brazil and Argentina.

The *cruzado* was the currency of Brazil from 1986 to 1989. It was replaced in 1989 by the *cruzado novo* at a rate of 1000 *cruzados* = 1 *cruzado novo*.

Santos Beach, approximately fifty miles from São Paulo, is home to the world's longest landscaped oceanfront garden, which runs parallel to the four-mile-long beach.

"Summer Is Fleeting"

Go is a board game often described as the Asian version of chess. It is believed to have originated in China thousands of years ago. Go is considered to be one of the world's foremost games of strategy and skill.

Vigor panties - Vigor is the brand name of a line of underwear sold in Korea.

Breathless, a 1960 French film written and directed by Jean-Luc Godard was one of the earliest, most influential examples of French New Wave cinema.

Namhan Fortress is approximately fifteen miles southeast of Seoul. The fortress, which is seven and a half miles long, contains fortifications that date back to the 17th century, and a number of temples.

Emma Bovary is the heroine of Gustav Flaubert's 1856 novel, *Madame Bovary*.

Double eyelids have a crease above the eye, which makes the eye look larger. Single lid eyes have no crease line when you open your eyes. Some Asian women undergo plastic surgery to create a double eyelid.

Oray, in Korean, is two characters: "oh" and "ray." "Ray" means "to come." In Korean, the numbers 1, 2, 3, 4, 5 are pronounced "il," "ee," "sam," "sa," "oh." Thus, Oh-ray means "fifth to come," and Il-ray means "first to come."

The *Hannam Bridge* is a girder bridge over the Han River. It connects Gangnam-gu and Yongsan-gu.

The *Kyobo Building* is a modern 22-story high-rise building in Seoul.

"In My Life"

Ewha Womans University is a private women's university in Seoul, South Korea founded in 1886 by an American Methodist missionary. It is the world's largest female educational institute and one of the most prestigious universities in South Korea. While the lack of an apostrophe in "Womans University" is unconventional, it was common usage in the past. The early founders of the college thought that every woman was to be respected and to promote this idea, they chose the word "woman" to avoid lumping students together under the word "women."

Sinchon is a district of Seoul known for its numerous universities including Ewha Womans University.

Susan Brink's Arirang is a 1991 film in which a Korean orphan is adopted by a Swedish couple and renamed Susan. Her new parents are very abusive and Susan unsuccessfully attempts suicide. *Arirang* is a Korean folk song often considered the unofficial national anthem of Korea. Many versions of the song describe the travails encountered by the subject of the song while crossing a mountain pass.

Korean Voices Series

Strong Wind At Mishi Pass
Poems by Tong-gyu Hwang
Translated by Seong-kon Kim & Dennis Maloney
Volume 4   1-893996-10-7   118 pages $15.00

A Sketch of the Fading Sun
Stories of Wan-suh Park
Translated by Hyun-jae Yee Sallee
VOLUME 3   1-877727-93-8   200 PAGES $15.00

Heart's Agony: Selected Poems of Chiha Kim
Translated by Won-chun Kim and James Han
VOLUME 2   1-877727-84-9   128 PAGES $14.00

The Snowy Road: An Anthology of Korean Fiction
Translated by Hyun-jae Yee Sallee
VOLUME 1   1-877727-19-9   168 PAGES $12.00